# *Bleed*

**By Marston Glenn**

**nzambi press**
**los angeles**
**2014**

Cover art by Jeffrey Gorski

Library of Congress Cataloging-in-Publication Data

Glenn, Marston, 1989-

Bleed/Marston Glenn

58 p. 21.6 cm. by 27.9 cm.

ISBN 978-1-312-26459-5

## Acknowledgments

I would like to thank Leopold Froehlich and Jason Buhrmester for helping with the book's design and editing. Thanks to Morgan Farrington for helping with plot ideas when I had writer's block. Thank you to Allison Bergson for helping with plot points and providing moral support. And thank you Cooper for getting me into zombies in the first place.

*For my father.*

# Saved By the Past

A ndrew Plumb lay on his bed and tossed a football over his head. His team's record was 7-1 and tomorrow would be the last game of the season. Throwing the football was a ritual for Andrew. It gave him an edge. Even if they lost, Andrew was still one of the most-scouted quarterbacks in the nation. But ever since he was in high school, he knew he wanted to be a microbiologist. Early on, Andrew met Dr. Strasborg. His father passed away a year before and the doctor became a father figure to Andrew.

"You can call me any time, day or night," Dr. Strasborg said. "We're a team now."

Andrew had blond hair. His face was chiseled but thin and his chin was small. He knew most of the cheerleaders at his high school had a crush on him and he soaked up as much of the attention as he could. They cheered for him and brought him gifts before games. The clock hit 11:00 p.m. Andrew turned off the bedside lamp and pulled the blanket over his head. He held the football in his armpit and closed his eyes.

He woke up at seven. After he showered he went into the kitchen. His mother placed his breakfast on the table and he enjoyed the eggs, bacon and toast.

That night the bright lights around the football field surrounded Andrew. Near the end of the fourth quarter the game was tied 27-27.

"Andrew, Andrew, he's our man, if he can't do it, no one can."

Andrew looked up at the scoreboard. He then looked at the crowd who stood and cheered and knew he needed this touchdown to win the game. He hiked the ball. His favorite wide receiver and best friend, Laurence, sprinted down the field.

•

Laurence and Andrew played video games and stared at the television with large eyes. Their fingers moved precisely around the controllers.

"Andrew!" yelled his mom. "The cookies are ready. Pause the game!"

Andrew put down the controller and stood up.

"Race you to the kitchen," he said.

They both sprinted to the other room.

"What did I say about running, Andrew?"

She picked him up.

"No running in the house."

•

Laurence sprinted down the field. Andrew threw the ball. Laurence watched as it moved closer in his direction.

*You got this*, Laurence thought.

The football was at the center of his sight, the bright night bordered the ball, and the lights shined around his periphery. The ball closed in. It was a couple feet from his hands when Laurence saw black. He was leveled by a player on the opposing team. The referees threw their penalty flags and the hit knocked Laurence unconscious. Andrew took off his helmet and sprinted toward the two players. The stadium's lights were in his eyes. Laurence had not moved. The other player's helmet was off and his face was near Laurence's neck as it jerked side to side like eyes watching a tennis match. He turned around and stared at Andrew, who was ten yards away. Andrew noticed the player had a tint of green on his white skin. The player turned back to Laurence and continued the motion.

"What the hell?" said Andrew.

The game ended with a whistle. The fans stood up to get a better view. Some of them yelled for the player to get off Laurence. Andrew noticed there was blood on his friend's jersey. He stood still. His coach and team ran past Andrew. They huddled around the two players on the ground. The other teams coach ran over.

"Fisher! Get off that boy!"

The coach grabbed the player by the collar and pulled him off Laurence. The coach saw the blood.

"Oh my god." His hand covered his mouth. "Fisher, what have you done?"

The player growled and breathed heavily, saliva dropped from his lower lip. His blond hair contrasted with his green skin. He had red eyes with lines of yellow, which shot out like bullets. He bit into the coach's hand. The coach fell on the grass. Fisher's team tackled the player.

The stadium lights shined on the crowd and the two teams. The audience was still. None of them had encountered anything so horrific at a football game.

A lower drum of feet could be heard about 150 yards beyond the school bleachers.

Laurence turned his head. He saw through foggy vision numerous silhouetted bodies. They marched toward him. Laurence's eyes closed. The audience had also turned around to see what was behind them. Their eyes, unaccustomed to the dark, strained to see who was there.

The night before, Andrew imagined his team and coach picking him up after throwing the winning catch. The hands would have felt like a giant bed.

"It's about time," he said.

But now reality struck him. A girl screamed in the bleachers. Laurence's girlfriend, Betsy, cried on her mother's shoulder. Her father wrapped his arms around her.

A few women gasped.

"Who are they?" asked one woman.

The monsters at the front of the pack were in plain sight. They all had green faces and walked toward the field. The demons swayed and limped onward. The audience ran down the bleachers. Some ran straight for their cars, others ran for their children. When the infected reached the bleachers, some walked around, some walked through, and some climbed toward their meal. They moved quicker the closer they got to the humans.

Andrew looked at the undead. People ran past him toward their cars. He saw one of the creatures grab his girlfriend, Denice. Andrew ran to her. The zombie tackled Denice to the ground. Andrew took his helmet in his right hand and beat the zombie in the back of the head. The zombie fell over and Denice curled up like a dead spider.

Andrew grabbed and tugged at her arm. Denice's hands were shaking. She would not stand up.

"Denice, stop it, stupid. Move. Come on."

Her eyebrows arched into a look of worry as she watched him. She got up but could not run as fast as Andrew. He pulled her in the direction of the high school's science building. Orange lights were bolted on the red walls. They lit up a walkway that was paved around the building. The sky was dark blue with a couple of stars overhead.

Andrew kicked open the front door. A large wooden bench had blocked it. Once inside Andrew blocked the door again. He heard moans from outside. They scratched at the door's smooth white paint.

"That won't hold them for long," said Andrew. "Come on—we need to find a safe place. A place they can't go."

They ran down the long white hall that resembled a hospital ward. Bright white lights hung from the ceiling. Classical music played over the speakers.

"Andrew, what's going on?" Denice asked.

A large thud down the hall reverberated on the walls.

"I wish I had a gun," Andrew said.

"That would be helpful," said a voice.

A man appeared from the hallway to the left of Andrew and Denice. Nicholas Lauren wore a white lab coat and donned circular spectacles with thin rims. Under the lab coat he wore a black suit. Underneath the suit he wore a base white dress shirt with straight and very thin beige stripes.

"Hurry," he said.

He turned and ran back down the hallway. Andrew and Denice were led inside the school's laboratory. The walls were white. Three large tables were spaced ten feet from one another. The tables' surfaces gleamed black and the foundations were light brown. The tiled floor was light gray. The lights that hung above them were long, thin and bright.

In the corner of the room was a 28-year-old woman. She was tall and slim and had long dark hair that touched the top of her buttocks. Her face was round, her cheeks were cushioned, and her nose was small and a little wide.

"I have looked at the virus chromosomes," Nicholas said. He moved the chair to fix the door shut and then looked into a microscope. "It's not like anything I've seen before." His mouth was open and his mind wandered.

"And?" asked Andrew.

"Basically, the organism enters the body and causes white blood cells to rush forth and fight the infection. In this respect, leukemia comes to my mind. The large number of white blood cells effectively and quickly kills the human host. Then, I believe, the infection spreads through the host's body. Simply put, it's like a virus that takes over a cell. Only this virus invades and controls the cell. I can't do anything to stop it."

Kelsey, the woman standing next to Nicholas, looked at him.

"We still need to survive, and it's as you said: None of this is going to help," said Kelsey.

"You got it," said Nicholas.

•

Nicholas woke up. The sunlight was on his bed. Finally a layer of warmth was on his eyelids. He opened his eyes. He sat on his bed and reached for his planner. Today's date was listed at the top left corner, "Oct. 2" and written just below in all caps was, "BIRTHDAY!" He looked lower on the calendar and saw that at seven p.m. he had written, "Meet Kelsey." He wondered who she was.

He walked down the stairs and placed two pieces of wheat bread in the toaster. He picked up a magazine written and edited specifically for molecular biologists. He read about Tuberculosis and the difficulties of global eradication. He usually read science magazines but when he dared he read *Playboy*. His Christian parents woke up at ten so that left him enough time to read a few articles.

•

Kelsey watched Nicholas, who had one eye on the

microscope. A few hours earlier, Nicholas brought her to a movie theater, which was then overrun by the creatures.

A loud bang sounded at the door. Denice looked at Andrew and pulled her head to his chest. Her arms wrapped around him.

"It's going to be okay," said Andrew.

He kissed her head.

"It'll all be over soon," he said.

He knew she couldn't survive much longer.

*What would be the quickest way?* he thought.

He got up from the seat and moved to the door. Her arms slid off him. Andrew looked at the chair that helped hold the door shut. The wooden pillars were cracking. The door shook violently.

"The door knob is going and the chair is breaking, too. They'll be here any second," said Andrew.

"All right. There's nothing else I can do," Nicholas said. "Let's go."

"Go through the vent. I'll hold them," said Andrew.

The door handle broke, and only the chair held the door in place. They heard the wood cracking. He looked at Denice.

"I need you to follow Nick, okay?"

"Okay, Denice, time to move," said Nicholas.

She nodded her head and stood up. The chair broke. Andrew pushed on the door. He couldn't hold the door any longer. It swung open and slammed into the wall. At least 15 heads sprinted into the laboratory.

•

A boy was in an elevator. The doors opened.

"Dr. Strasborg." Andrew walked into the laboratory. "Dr.

Strasborg." He looked around.

He closed the door behind him. The lights were on. He smiled and looked at the posters on the wall. Laboratory equipment was strewn across a table in the center of the room. Beakers were held up with clear and colored fluid inside. A microscope was on a black table. In the corner was a white board. He looked closely and read: "Infection takes control of the host's body."

The door opened. Someone was behind Andrew.

"Hey, Dr. Strasborg," said Andrew.

"Hello, Andrew."

He walked to the boy. He had on a white lab coat.

"How's it going? How is your mom?"

"Oh, she's okay," said Andrew.

Dr. Strasborg looked at the board behind Andrew.

"There are a lot of things we don't know, but that's what makes this job more exciting. To get to the bottom of it."

.

Andrew ran from the horde of zombies behind him. Kelsey, Nicholas and Denice were already in the ventilation shaft. The zombies were five feet away, scratching at air and almost grabbing his skin. He jumped onto the black surface of the table. The vent was 11 feet above the table and a few feet to the left. The survivors had used a stool to climb up but it had been kicked over. Andrew would have to jump.

He jumped three feet in the air, using his football skills. The ends of his fingers clung to the ventilation shaft. He pulled himself up and saw Denice staring at him in horror.

"Did they bite you?" she asked.

"No," he replied.

They moved through the vents quickly.

"We're going to have to reach the roof. Nowhere else is safe." Nicholas said. He looked through the vent slips as he crawled forward. "The school is flooded with those things."

"Get to the roof," Andrew said.

"Uh, we have a problem," said Nicholas.

"What is it?" Kelsey asked.

"We'll need to go up the vent," said Nicholas.

"What do you mean?" Kelsey asked.

"Well, look here," Nicholas said.

The vent went upward.

"We're going to need someone to lift the others up to the roof," said Nicholas.

"But the last person won't make it," said Kelsey.

"We'll pull him up," said Nicholas.

"Hurry up," said Andrew.

Nicholas stood in the vent. He was very skinny and could barely pick up Kelsey. He grabbed her foot and lifted her toward the sky. She pushed open the vent and climbed onto the roof.

"No one is up here," said Kelsey.

"Okay, Denice. Go," said Andrew.

"Okay," said Denice. "I'm ready."

Her red polished heels hit Nicholas' hand. He pushed her up and Kelsey grabbed Denice's right hand. Her other hand grabbed the thin top of the ventilation shaft.

Nicholas went up, and then Andrew. On the roof there was a staircase that led up to them. There was a loud bang on the other side of the door.

"They're coming," said Andrew.

"Oh my god," Denice said.

She held on to Andrew.

"Where do we go?" asked Denice.

"We wait," said Nicholas. "We wait for them."

"No," said Andrew. "There has to be another way." He looked around. "I think…."

Andrew looked over the side of the building. They were five stories high.

"I think we should all jump," said Andrew.

"No," said Nicholas. "There has to be…." He looked at the edge of the building. "If we cling our hands to the side of the building and drop to the story below the roof. We can stand on the ledge."

"I'll go first," said Denice.

She held onto the edge of the roof, which was stone, and lowered herself to the level below. She stayed close to the wall so her cheek touched the brick. Kelsey let herself down and then Andrew went down. All but Nicholas were safe on the ledge.

The zombies broke through the roof door.

"Shit," Nicholas said.

The zombies ran at Nicholas.

"You can make it," Andrew said. "Hurry!"

Nicholas lowered himself at the roof's ledge. The first zombie was five feet away from him. The top half of Nicholas' face was still above the roof. He looked at the monsters that ran at him. One of the creature's eye sockets was empty and his scalp was almost bald. He had wiry black hair, and his lips were turned up in a grin. Nicholas lowered himself. The zombie ran off the roof a second later.

"Holy shit. I can't believe…I'm alive," Nicholas said.

Gunshots were heard above them. Zombies yelled. Andrew lifted his head above the roof. His eyes widened.

"Who is it, Andrew?" Denice asked.

"Dr. Strasborg?" Andrew said.

A man with black hair, chiseled face and thin build stood in front of the door smoking a cigarette. His doctor's coat flew in the wind. A lightning bolt lit up his face.

"Andrew," he said. "We don't have time. Come on."

# Be Cold to Strangers

Pete was in his car speeding to the scene. He skidded to a stop in front of the hospital. He looked around the parking lot and saw other patrol cars. People ran out of the hospital screaming.

"This is worse than a 10-10."

Pete ran inside. He heard shots fired. He ran up to the third floor. His partners shot at the monsters. Pete pulled his weapon out of the holster. He fired at the ones eating the patients who were too injured to run. Pete's last bullet hit a fellow officer in the shoulder.

"Oh, shit. Sorry, Tony."

"Goddamn it. Learn to aim, Pete."

Pete fired three more shots. They each hit the head of a zombie. Even though he couldn't believe it, subconsciously he knew what they were and he knew where to shoot them.

"Get me out of here," Tony said. "Hell's on earth."

He picked up Tony and put him on his shoulders. Pete walked down the stairs and got his friend outside.

"What's happening?" asked Tony.

"I know as much as you," said Pete.

"It's some sort of virus." He clenched his eyes.

"Medic, get him to a hospital that isn't…you know, *fucked*."

An EMT put Tony on a stretcher and then into an ambulance.

"I'll see you soon," Pete said.

Tony gave him a thumbs up.

Pete watched the hospital burn at its top two levels. People ran from the hospital entrance. A zombie tackled a woman. She screamed in agony and felt for her scalp, which had just been ripped off by the zombie's teeth. Pete got in his patrol car and drove away. He drove home and was greeted by his wife when he walked through the front door.

"Are you okay?" he asked.

"Yeah," she said. "Why wouldn't I? What's wrong?"

"Something happened. At the hospital, there was an infection. A lot of people died. We can't stop it."

"Oh my god. What kind of infection?"

"I don't know. Get in the basement."

His wife moved quickly to the basement. Pete turned all three locks on the basement door. There was a small window there that wasn't big enough to fit a body through. Pete and Anne peered through the window and saw people running from creatures who screamed and spit blood from their mouths.

"If they break in, we leave through the tunnels," said Pete.

He looked over at a tunnel in his basement. The door was sealed by a latch.

"Okay."

They sat there until night draped over them. The stars in the sky illuminated the street. The zombies walked around, but to Pete and his wife they looked just like shadows until Anne started to cry.

"Hey, it's okay," said Pete.

"No, it's not," said Anne.

"Okay, maybe it's not."

"Yeah."

"We're going to make it through this, okay? We've got a lot of food and this place is practically a castle."

"I guess you're right. It's just my family. I hope they're okay."

"They're probably holed up just like us. All right? I'm going to go and get us some food. Stay here."

Anne nodded her head.

He walked up the stairs and unlocked the door. The house was dark. He walked to the kitchen as carefully as he could. He spotted a head moving by the window. The creature walked into his backyard. Pete went to the cupboard and took some bread. He then took turkey from the refrigerator. He returned downstairs with the food.

"Thanks."

"I couldn't bring more because they were outside the house. We'll just have to risk it every now and then. Maybe when things calm down we'll bring all the food down to the basement. I saved the cans for tomorrow because the food in the refrigerator is going to go bad."

They went to sleep shortly after eating. Pete woke up early in the morning. The sun couldn't be seen and the sky was gray. Dew lay on the window, on the grass, and on the plants. The creatures still stumbled around outside.

"Not much has changed." He looked at his gun rack. "There are probably more of them out there then I can take."

He looked at Anne. He loved her more than anything in the world. He walked over to the gun rack.

*My job is to keep her safe. Keep us safe.*

Time passed through the day. He looked at Anne. A small part of her blonde hair was on her face. He heard a screeching in the street. A car crashed into multiple zombies and then remained still. The zombies around the neighborhood started to swarm the car. The driver's door opened and pushed the zombies out of the way. A shotgun fired. The man ran forward firing shot after shot.

"He's going to die out there," said Pete.

"Can't we do something?" asked Anne.

Pete ran for his gun rack and grabbed his M4A1. He went up the stairs and unlocked the door.

"Wait here."

He closed the door and ran to a window. He pushed the gun through the glass. Shots rang out. The man with the shotgun stopped firing. The zombies were all dead.

"Over here," said Pete.

The man ran to the front door. Pete unlocked the door.

"Thank you."

"What's your name?"

"Josh."

He was Latino. Bald and short.

"Come to our basement. My wife is down there, too."

"It's much appreciated."

Pete led the way to the basement.

"Now hold on just a second. How much food can you carry?"

After a few minutes Pete and Josh walked down the stairs of the basement carrying canned foods and water bottles from the kitchen. Pete locked the door after he placed the grocery bags on the ground.

"So what brings you here?" asked Pete.

"I was driving to see my grandmother. I needed to know she was okay," said Josh. "I know you probably think I'm dumb for leaving my house, but I just had to know."

"I don't think you're crazy," said Pete. "I think you're brave for trying to find your grandmother."

"Really?" asked Josh. "She lives a couple blocks down."

"I'll help you find her."

"Thank you. Thank you so much."

He hugged Pete.

"We'll leave tomorrow when the sun is up," said Pete. "For now, let's get some rest. There's an extra blanket for you over there."

Pete pointed to the corner of the room. Josh moved over and got the blanket. Pete and Anne rolled up next to each other.

*Are there really such kind people in the world?* thought Josh.

"We'll wake you in the morning," said Pete.

The next morning they all stood behind the front door.

"I'm watching point, Anne you watch the left, and Josh you got my right side. We go on three. Ready? One. Two. *Three.*"

Pete opened the door and shot a zombie. They moved past their green lawn and garden gnomes all the while taking down the infected. When they reached the car, Pete got in the driver's seat.

"Okay. Which way?"

A few zombies surrounded the car but there weren't many around since Josh showed up. They growled and hissed at the humans.

"It's just straight down this street for a mile."

They drove. The white houses on either side were not destroyed yet. Things seemed almost normal except for the monsters who appeared on the sidewalks, lawns and patios. Some of the windows were broken and some of the smaller white picket fences were trampled. It was as if someone had ruined the American dream. Eventually, they made it to the house.

"What are the threats when we get in there?" asked Pete.

"What do you mean?" asked Josh.

"He means who is in there? Beside your grandma. Who else could be infected?" asked Anne.

"First of all, my grandma isn't infected. Every Tuesday and Thursday she has a nurse come over. She takes care of her cleaning and makes sure my grandma is taking her medicine."

"Okay," said Pete. "We get in, get your grandmother and get out."

"Okay."

Anne nodded her head.

The car doors opened and they ran up the brick walkway. The front door was unlocked.

"Grandma?" said Josh.

He ran up the staircase. Pete and Anne looked around the first floor of the house. Pete walked through a room with two sofas and a glossy hardwood floor. He then walked into the kitchen, which had white walls and a white tiled floor. Little parakeet salt-and-pepper shakers were on the counter.

"Hello?"

Anne walked up the stairs. As she walked down the hall a closet rumbled. She looked at it. She started to point her gun up when a tall woman with dreadlocks burst from the door. Her eyes were green and red. She moved quickly and sunk her teeth into Anne's neck. Anne fired a shot into the wall as she cried and screamed.

# Love at First Bite

The bride wore a hand-knit white wedding dress. The train of the dress extended five feet behind her. A little girl was under the slack of the dress. She held her hands up as she walked behind the bride. The short and skinny bride had wavy blonde hair that fell just past her shoulders. Jim, the groom, liked that her smile gave away an innocent intelligence. Her nose was short and pointed up. Her cheeks went out as if she had a slight allergic reaction and they were always rosy. Her name was Sylvia and she smiled slightly at her husband as she walked down the aisle with her father.

The groom had short hair spiked with gel. He was tall and his shoulders were broad. He smiled and looked down at his feet. He then looked up at her with a smile. His eyes reflected the light from the sun. Jim lifted his head and straightened his posture.

When she reached the stage, the little girl walked to the first line of chairs, where the onlookers sat and watched. The train of the dress pulled with the little girl, so the bride had to hold on to the back of the dress with her right hand.

"Sorry," the groom's mother said.

She picked up the little girl and sat down. The woman waved her hand quickly as if to say *Don't look at me*. Her handkerchief dotted her eye.

The pastor stood between the bride and the groom. He was taller and skinnier than Jim. Gray hair grew from the sides of his head. He wore bifocals that glimmered in the sun when he looked down at the Bible.

"We gather here today to celebrate the holy communion of marriage," he said.

The voice boomed past the onlookers, on the grass, over the cliffside and into the forest.

"They are here out of love. A thing which is holy in itself."

Jim's parents' eyes watered. They leaned their heads and bodies together. Jim looked at Sylvia. He could see the cliffside, the ocean and the sun behind her. The sun started to set and the sky was orange from the horizon to the top and dark blue on the other side. Behind Sylvia were the bridesmaids, who stood between the background and foreground of the moment. Their dresses were the color of a purple beet and her father—who wore a black suit—stood a few feet behind and to the right of Sylvia.

The marriage was finalized after an hour and a half. The punch was served on a table with a white tablecloth. The punch bowl was made of glass and had designs of roses, with rose stems and rose leafs on it. The bowl resembled a glass flower. There were chocolate roses placed on the white tables where the guests sat. There were also assortments of flowers at the center of the tables.

Jim found the location with his brother Simon. They flew up and down the coast of Maine until they found the ideal place on a cliffside in the Hancock area. The land was next to a cliff about 100 yards above sea level. At the top of the cliff was lush grass that reached the shadows of the forest farther inland.

One boy ran around the tables and guests. He was shorter than the tables and chairs and he held an action figure in his right hand. His arm was nearly aligned to the horizon as he imagined his flying action figure. He mimicked the sounds of a fighter jet engine as he ran on the grass and looked back at his nanny, who a few minutes before had told him not to wander. The boy made the sound of a missile traveling through the air and finally exploding. He then ran toward the forest.

"Jaime, don't do that!" said the nanny.

She ran toward him, but as she reached the edge of the forest he was already inside. She looked into the forest before entering. At the edge of the trees, the light was more abundant but the farther she looked in the forest, the more the light dimmed, until she could see only black.

"You're never going to catch me," he said. The voice echoed off the trees, but originated somewhere to her left.

"Jaime, where are you?" She stepped into the forest. She walked past bushes close to her and then ducked under a branch. The grass was sparse and the ground was a combination of dirt and mud. Mud got on her shoes from the ground and stained her dress.

She walked to a small clearing in the forest. A small circle of light from the sun poked through the trees. The bushes and trees circled them. Thick green grass grew under the circle of light. The sun's light showed the dust in the air.

She heard the snap of a twig behind her. She turned around,

"Jaime?" She looked into the forest. She saw a person's silhouette standing behind a tree. The head, the shoulders and the slanted half of the body were visible. The broad shoulders and long face indicated to her that the person was a man.

"Is that you?" Her eyes squinted as her heart quickened.

"*Rawr!*" Jaime said.

He was behind her.

"Jaime! You scared me."

"Sorry."

"Come on." She pulled his arm. "Let's go back to the party."

The nanny looked at the location where she had seen the figure. The silhouette was gone.

"Don't ever run off like that again."

They walked on the grass with her pulling Jaime's arm through the forest.

"I would like to give a toast," said Simon. He had blond buzzed hair. One could see his scalp beneath the strands of hair.

The speech finished. Old women at the back of the party smiled as they commented on the speech. Simon stood on the cliffside. Jim walked up to him.

"So," said Jim.

"So," said Simon.

"You still love her, don't you?"

"Yes."

He looked at the orange sky.

"I never thought you would get married before me, that's for sure," said Simon.

"What are you doing?" asked Jim. "You come to my wedding…"

Simon laughed.

"You sound like Mom."

"You're nothing but pathetic."

Jim walked away. The sun had set and the stars shined silver. They reflected off the ocean water. Jim looked back and saw his brother was not where they had just talked. Jim ran to the edge of the cliff. He looked over and saw his brother's corpse on the rocks at the bottom. Jim put his hands over his mouth as tears dribbled down. He walked back to the party and grabbed his wife's hand. They walked toward the line of parked golf carts.

"Jim, what's going on?"

She was pulled by him.

"Jim."

She pulled her hand away and stopped.

His hands were open, stiff and straight. He held them on both sides of his nose.

"Sylvia, we need to go."

He leaned down and moved his face closer to hers.

"I'll explain at the parking lot, okay?" His eyes were watered and red.

"Okay, okay."

They got into the golf cart and drove on the dirt road, where they disappeared from sight.

As they drove they heard sounds in the forest. It seemed to Jim that a wolf or something had been following them but was deep in the forest and past his vision. Sylvia held on to Jim and placed her face on his biceps.

"What is that sound?"

She held him tight. He looked at her and then up at the woods on the right side from the road.

"It's just an animal following our lights or going the same way as us."

He heard a twig snap behind a bush near them. He looked at her.

"I know." Her sweater covered her mouth.

He kissed the top of her head and then looked at the road. He pressed the gas pedal harder. Three minutes later, a woman screamed ahead of the golf cart and to their left.

"What was that?" Sylvia asked. Her voice trembled and was high-pitched. "Jim?"

"Stay here."

He stopped the golf cart. He got off and looked into the woods to the left of the road. He saw a cabin with orange lights on the inside. He squinted his eyes and walked off the dirt road. He moved between the bushes. He walked closer to the cabin. When he was six feet from the door he noticed it was slightly ajar. The open slit let out orange light that illuminated a cone on the forest ground. He grabbed the doorknob. The door creaked open slowly. He let go and the door opened itself. He saw a figure inside the cabin. He did not hear the movement a few feet behind him. A woman lay motionless on the floor. Jim moved inside the cabin. His shoes tapped the floorboards. The woman struggled to break the grip of the ropes around her.

He kneeled at her side. She was young and wore a turquoise nightgown. Her shoes were off and her feet were muddy. She looked at Jim and then behind him.

*Save her*, Jim thought.

"Okay, okay."

He breathed and worked on loosening the knot on her left wrist. The rope was thick and multiple knots were made for each limb. He had undone the first one when he heard a voice behind him.

"Get your hands off my wife!" The man was skinny with a thin face and big eyes. Mud was on his overalls and face. A shovel was in his right hand. "Did you hear me?"

"No. Yes. Yes, I heard you."

Jim's vision blurred, but at the center was the man with the shovel. Jim grasped for air and put his hand to his chest as he walked for the door.

"My wife and I," Jim said. He reached the doorframe.

The man was four feet from him.

"We were making sure everything was okay."

The woman behind him laughed. He passed through the door and was outside the cottage. A shock ran through his body.

"I have to get to my wife," Jim said, as he ran to the golf cart.

"Why don't you come inside and I'll get you some coffee?"

Jim neared the golf cart.

"What happened? Are you okay? Jim?" asked Sylvia.

"Yeah," he said. "His wife and him were having some sort of party or something."

He stepped in the golf cart and pressed the pedal. The man watched the golf cart pass. "He's gone," Jim said. "My brother is gone. He killed himself."

"Oh my god."

Tears filled his eyes. The golf cart stopped. He cried in his lap.

"I'm fine. I'm fine. I'm fine."

"Sweetie, I don't know his reasons, but I know he had reasons. You need to calm down."

"Calm down? Calm down? I don't need to calm down."

"Okay, okay, I understand," she said. "Maybe now isn't the time."

"Time for what?" he replied

"Never mind," said Sylvia.

He put his hand on her back and pulled her to his chest. Her tears fell like tiny blue marbles. As they drove on there was another rustle to the right. This time it was close to the golf cart. A person jumped from the bushes; her face was dark green. Parts of her flesh were falling off her face as she screamed. It was the nanny who took care of Jaime. She grabbed Sylvia and bit her neck. The nanny dragged her off the golf cart with her teeth and arms. The dust kicked up and was lit by the golf cart's brake lights. Jim stopped his golf cart and ran toward the monster. He kicked the back of her head. She fell off of Sylvia and looked at Jim as she screamed and gurgled Sylvia's blood. Jim lifted his shoe and stomped her face. He then dropped down to Sylvia and looked at her. She gurgled blood and looked at the stars. The top of her bright blue eyes shined neon from the moonlight.

"Oh no, oh no, no, no. You can't die, Syl. You can't die."

She coughed blood that dripped on her chin. She looked at him.

"I have nothing," he said. "There is only you. There is only you." He cried between her breast and arm.

Sylvia stared at the stars. Her eyes and her body did not move.

"Okay, okay."

He picked her up, put her in the golf cart, and drove toward the cabin.

# A Passion to Survive

D an was with his girlfriend at a diner.

"Do you love me?" asked Tricia.

"Of course I do," said Dan.

"I don't believe you," said Tricia.

"It's true as true gets. I couldn't love you anymore than I do now. I couldn't love anybody more than I love you," said Dan.

"Aww," said Tricia. "That's sweet."

She took a sip of her chocolate malt. The waiter walked past them in a bright pink dress. She had blonde hair and was wearing a white apron.

"What made you ask such a thing?"

"You know, boys in the past I thought I loved really didn't treat me well. So, I'm just afraid it'll happen again."

"I'll never leave you," he said. "Could I get a check, please?"

"Sure, sweetheart."

Dan had brown hair. Tricia had blonde hair and a thin build. She had big breasts. Dan had scruff and a mean look to him. He was six foot two. She was five foot seven.

"You know, you got me thinking crazy things. I've never been with a woman like you."

"You're just as sweet as punch."

They walked out of the diner to his car. They drove to the movies. The film was about a hero who rescued his wife and children from a terrible disease. When the movie was over they drove back to his place. The next morning they woke up and got breakfast. He dropped her off at her place and went to work. He worked as an accountant.

"Hey," said Ted.

Dan sat at his desk. Ted stood outside his cubicle.

"Hey," said Dan.

"Did you hear about the rabies outbreak in Wisconsin?"

"No, I haven't heard about it."

"It's pretty bad and it's spreading to humans pretty quickly," said Ted.

"Jesus. Are you serious?"

"Serious."

"Does the CDC have it under control?"

"They've quarantined the area. There's no cure for it at the moment."

"Oh my god. Isn't there a rabies shot they can give them?"

"It's not working. Whatever it is. It's not normal rabies."

"Wow, I hope they are okay."

"Me, too, I'll see you for dinner later?"

"Yeah, yeah."

Dan left for home after work. He checked his dog Biscuit for rabies.

"You okay, boy?" asked Dan. "Yeah, you're okay."

Dan pet his dog and massaged his mouth. Biscuit barked.

"You want to go for a walk?"

The dog barked again.

"I'm not sure I can understand you."

The dog barked.

"You'd rather stay home?"

The dog barked.

"Okay, then. We can stay home."

Dan's phone rang. He picked up.

"Hello?"

"Hey," said Ted. "Want to go to Wild Buffalo Sports Bar?"

"Sure, I was just checking Biscuit for rabies."

"Is he okay?" asked Ted.

"Yeah, he's fine. Any more news on the rabies outbreak?"

"They've got the place quarantined and they are treating the sick. A corporation called Merricorp found a cure. That's all I know."

"Okay, good."

Dan drove over to the bar. He sat down next to Ted. He had short blond hair and blue eyes.

"Hey, look at that one over there," said Ted.

He pointed to a blonde with a big butt.

"She looks tasty," said Dan.

"You bet your ass she does. Do you think I should go over there and talk to her?"

"Yeah, definitely."

Ted walked over to the blonde woman. Dan watched her walk away from Ted. Ted came back to the table.

"Not interested?" said Dan.

"Clearly. How's your girl?"

"I think I'm in love with her."

"That's great, man. Now if only we could find you a better girl. How about that one?"

He pointed to a brunette who was talking to her friends.

"Quit being a jackass. I feel bad for those rabies victims."

"God, you're boring. Look around you. You're swimming in women and all you can think about is Wisconsin?"

They both laughed.

"It's serious," said Dan.

"Yeah, whatever. When I was in the twelfth grade there was this super hot Spanish teacher named Señorita Lupe. So I played it cool and she would just walk over to me and lean down so I could see her breasts and help me with my Spanish. She would get really close so we would be touching."

"And?"

"And I fucked her."

"You know what you do? You objectify women."

"No, I don't."

"Yeah, you do."

"I just love pussy, that's all."

"Anyways, the drinks here were good tonight."

"Yeah, they were."

"I better get going."

"I hear you."

Dan left the bar and drove home. He lay in his bed. His phone vibrated. It was a text from Tricia.

"Meet me at the diner tomorrow for dinner?"

"Sure."

Dan woke up in the morning and went to work. He got off work at six. As he left the building a woman in the parking lot was crying.

"What's wrong?"

"They're dead. They're all dead."

He looked at the road. Cars sped past him way over the speed limit. He heard screams and sirens. He walked to the sidewalk and saw humans eating humans. People ran toward him. Dan ran to his car and quickly pulled out of the parking lot. His phone vibrated.

"Meet at the diner now! We need to leave."

Dan sped over to a grocery store. The parking lot was full. People left their cars in the driveway. Dan did the same. Horns honked and people ran in and out of the store with goods. Dan ran into the store and looked for canned food. He came across three cans of asparagus. He took them and ran out of the store. He got back in his car. He drove to the end of the driveway. He could turn left or he could go home, get his dog and leave. He turned right. His phone rang. He opened his glove compartment box and saw the pistol was still there. When he got home, he packed his clothes and all his food in two suitcases. He put them in his car and then went back for his dog. He put him in the passenger seat and drove off toward the forest.

# *Lazy Dayz*

T oday was a day just like any other, except he felt extremely depressed. Last week, he had been laid off as the marketing executive of a software company and ever since he had looked in the papers, called some contacts, and went through a lot of interviews. He hoped he would find a job in this downturn economy. He looked at the ceiling. His blankets were unusually warm.

*Did I forget to turn down the air conditioner?* He got up and looked at the air conditioner box. The LCD screen showed the temperature was set to 90 degrees. "That's why." He pressed the down button until the screen showed 80 degrees. "That'll feel better." He returned to bed.

He looked forward to the chili and rice his girlfriend Kaylie would bring over later. They had been together for three years and neither of them had cheated on the other.

He stared at his white ceiling and wondered how he would get another job. His brown hair contrasted the white pillow as he pondered his predicament. His body sunk into the bed since last night, which left an indentation. He turned his head left and saw his landline and a large digital clock that displayed the time in bright red numbers. The clock showed it was 1:30 p.m. He thought of the activities he could do when he would get up from bed. He could get a hot dog on the street, he could go Christmas shopping for Kaylie, or he could see his parents. He chose to stay in bed.

The sheets were wet with perspiration and his forehead was covered with beads of sweat, which dripped into his sideburns and past his temples. He got up and walked to the kitchen. He set the fire on his stove and put a hot dog in a pan. He wore red and black striped boxers and his forehead barely passed the wooden cupboard.

The hot dog cooked until it was golden and black. He plucked the dog out with silvery prongs and placed it on a plate. He opened the refrigerator and took out a pitcher of milk, which he poured into a glass. He brought his food to the table and sat down. His door opened but no one was there. He turned around and looked out his apartment window. There was another apartment building in front of his, a block away. The building was black and shined in the sun. He looked back at the door and a gust of wind rushed through. It hit his face and he could smell snow, cold air and a hint of pine. The door swung into the wall.

"Goddamn it." He quickly walked over and closed the door.

A few seconds later there was a knock. He smiled and opened the door. A tall and slim business woman stood in front of his door.

"No, that's not okay, Joseph. No, bring the boxes to me on Friday and I'll take a look myself."

She hung up the phone and looked at him.

"Hey honey," Kaylie said.

He smiled and pulled her in by the waist. She looked up at him and kissed him on the lips. She had long blonde hair, which was contained within a small ponytail. She sat down on a chair next to the table. She tapped her fingernails on the table in rapid succession.

"You're always moving. Can't you just relax for a couple of minutes? Slow down and just let things be?" said Kyle.

She laughed.

"Darling, if I *let things be*, as you say." Her hands gestured quotation marks. "I would not *be* in business. In fact, I would not *be* anything worth mentioning. I would *be* at the docks somewhere putting things in crates. Oh god, can you imagine?" She looked at her watch. "Anyways, who are you to say anything about relaxing? You're usually busy, too. It hurts me to see you like this. It really does. If my father were here he would say…oh, never mind. You've been so lethargic, dear, and you've been acting very strange."

He looked her in the eye.

"I'm trying, okay? I've been up and down this city the past week looking for a new job. I've done at least a dozen interviews and submitted over 16 résumés."

"And it's so beautiful to see you working hard. Oh, I have a meeting to get to. I'll see you tonight?"

"Yeah," he said.

She kissed him on the cheek.

"Here's the chili and rice you asked for. Don't get so down on yourself."

She walked through the door and the last thing he saw of her was the back of her black coat and her black dress pants.

"Bye." He looked at his food.

The outer layer was a white plastic bag. The middle layer contained a Styrofoam rice container underneath a square Styrofoam container, and on the inside was fried rice and chopped chicken breast. He opened the bag and looked inside. He then rewrapped the bag and placed it in his fridge. He went back to the dark wooden table and finished his hot dog.

He proceeded to stare at the wall for an hour. He looked at his watch and saw it was two p.m. He took a shower and put on his clothes. He sprayed on cologne and fixed his hair with gel. He put on a penny coat and blue jeans and went outside. He looked in front of him with a keen eye on the tall buildings. Snow and water dripped down their sides.

Last night, he had a strange dream where the world collapsed beneath him. There was no light, only black, and the image of buildings free-falling in front of him. He walked faster and hardened his face. He looked at other peoples' faces. The women looked like stone statues. He mimicked their expressions and admired their perseverance. He secretly longed to hold them but blocked the thought out of his mind. Such thoughts were distractions. He walked over to a newspaper container. He grabbed the metal bar and opened the box. He grabbed the newspaper and looked at the jobs section. He saw nothing that interested him. He went into a small diner. The peoples' faces were blurred, he looked at the waitress, smiled and looked down again. His groin jumped, his heart tightened, and his calf muscles did the same. He sat down at the table and let out a large sigh.

"What can I get for you?" asked the waitress.

He looked at her blue eyes. The physical sensation was back. Her black hair shined. "I'll have a water, please." He looked into her eyes to see if she gave a hint of any interest. She smiled back at him. His smile grew and he looked down at the menu.

"I need a little more time."

"Sure."

He got up and went to the bathroom.

*I want something constant in my life, something permanent. But every smile I give eventually turns into a frown. Every feeling I have changes into something else. And every job I take changes to something else. There is more to uncover. On the bright side, every frown I give turns into a smile and every job I lose is a new opportunity.*

He smiled because of his logical optimism. He washed his hands and returned to the table. The waitress returned with a smile.

"Are you ready?"

He put up one hand.

"Just the water. Thanks."

She turned to leave.

"Can I ask what you're doing tomorrow night? There's this great Italian restaurant about three blocks down from here."

The waitress blushed. "Sorry. I'm engaged." She showed her ring.

"That's a beautiful ring for a beautiful woman."

"Thank you."

She smiled, turned around and went back toward the kitchen—but not before turning around and smiling one more time. He smiled back. When she turned back around he stood up and walked out of the diner. He wondered who had heard what he said. He looked through the diner's windows and saw the waitress at a table occupied by a couple in their late 20s. Both were smiling and talking to her.

He walked down the street and pulled a toothpick out of his pocket. He rammed the wooden piece in the spaces between his teeth, into his gums.

*Bleed, goddamn it*, he thought.

He stopped himself.

*Kyle, you're better than that.*

He walked about three blocks further and then decided to go home.

*My girl is too stressed. Shut up already. You're the stressed one just as much as she's the stressed one. Traumatic stress is what psychologists call it and judging by the looks on peoples' faces, everyone in New York City has it.*

He walked quickly to his apartment and made it there in under 15 minutes. Once inside he checked his voicemail.

"Hi Kyle, this is John calling from the office of Dan Bloomberg. We have a message regarding your interview and résumé. Call us back when you get this during our business hours, eight a.m. to five p.m."

Kyle picked up the phone and called the number. A voice on the other side spoke in a light quick tone.

"Hello?" she said.

"Hi, I'm returning a call regarding my recent interview for the marketing position. My name is Kyle Warner."

"One moment, please."

Kyle heard white noise for a few seconds and then a man picked up the phone. "Hi, Mr. Warner, we were just talking about you. It is… unfortunate, your circumstances. We were just looking over your résumé and it is very impressive, to say the least. And even though we weren't planning on hiring we've made an exception."

"I understand. Thank you very much. This is quite a relief."

"We look forward to working with you. Come by tomorrow and we'll go over the details. You'll start Monday at eight a.m."

"Thank you again. I'll see you tomorrow."

Kyle smiled and hung up the phone.

*Could this day get any better?*

His phone rang again. He picked up. It was his girlfriend, Kaylie.

"Hey Kyle, I know you're working hard, which is why I wanted to have a movie night tonight. I'll bring the ice cream and you can bring the movie."

"Sounds great, How about *Frankenstein*? It's a classic."

"You know I hate scary movies."

"Okay. How about *Happy Gilmore*?"

"Okay. I'll see you tonight."

"Oh, by the way, I got a job in marketing for a multimillion-dollar company. They're called Taylor & Stein Corp. Just thought I'd let you know I'm not as broke as you think."

"Oh, babe. Congratulations! That's wonderful! I'll see you tonight, I have some news as well! But I'll wait till then. All right, I got to go. Love you."

"I love you."

Kyle looked at the wall again. His face was still. He stood up from the chair and walked to his room. He looked at his closet mirror and at the silver handle. He pulled the sliding door to the side. He grabbed his running shoes from the floor of the closet. He slid the door closed again, walked over to his dresser, and opened the middle drawer. He pulled out a white long-sleeved shirt, blue sweat pants and a black headband. He jogged out of his apartment building. His eyes were intent on the street in front of him. Some turned their heads and looked at the man who contrasted their black coats and black dress pants.

Dark gray and light gray clouds hung over head. The rain came down and people moved quickly out of the way, into bars and diners or to their cars and taxis. Kyle continued his run with a grin. His short spiked hair shined due to the mixture of water and gel.

*There is no god, there is only you.*

And with that he ran with his back facing his apartment. He looked at his watch. It read 3:16 p.m.

*I'll turn back at 3:45 p.m.*

His goal was set, and he knew he would accomplish it. A car to his right switched to the far left lane. Its tires continued to move left until it was on the wrong side. The car hit the curb and ran into a store window. The accident happened 20 feet in front of Kyle.

"Oh my," said a woman.

"Call 911," said someone else.

Kyle ran to the accident. Another car crashed into a street lamp and another car hit the first car that drove through the window. The driver in the first car fell out as he opened the door. A blond woman with stilettos ran to his side and knelt down. She put her head close to his mouth. The man lifted his head and bit a chunk of her neck. The woman screamed and fell to the ground. She held the wound shut with her hands.

"Help," she screamed.

Kyle heard a siren about three blocks to his left. The sound was in front of him, passed behind him and continued on. A woman was on her phone.

"Yes. He just bit her," she said. "There's blood everywhere."

# Surviving the End

D r. Strasborg helped Andrew, Nicholas, Kelsey and Denice escape their infected high school. They all sat in a gun store. Dr. Strasborg cleaned his two pistols. Night crept over them.

"Does anyone have any questions on how to use their gun?" said Dr. Strasborg.

"No," said Kelsey.

Nicholas shook his head.

"No," said Denice.

"No," said Andrew.

Kelsey had a hunting rifle, Nicholas had a pistol, Denice had a pistol and Andrew carried a shotgun.

"We haven't eaten for two days. We need food," said Denice.

"Andrew, Nicholas and I will get food in the morning. I want you to stay here. Hold down the fort," said Dr. Strasborg.

"Okay," said Denice.

Doctor Strasborg looked at the GPS device.

"There's a liquor store about a mile from here," said Dr. Strasborg.

They left in the morning because there was no power at night, making it difficult to see the zombies. If they used a flashlight it would draw attention. They left through the back door, which led to an alleyway. They made sure the girls locked the door and then headed for the main street. They walked down the street with their guns at the ready. Nicholas watched their backs, Dr. Strasborg took point and Andrew watched the sides. They stayed close to the buildings.

Eventually they made it to the liquor store. They stocked up on cookies, water and protein bars. Dr. Strasborg got a bottle of whiskey.

"Okay," said Dr. Strasborg. "Let's move."

There was a noise in the back of the liquor store. A hissing sound, which became an inhuman scream. The creature walked to the front of the store. Once the zombie saw the humans he ran at them. He had red eyes and black hair. He was shorter than Andrew. Andrew lifted his gun and fired two shots. One shot hit the zombie's chest and the other his head. There was a loud scream outside the store.

"They're coming," said Nicholas.

"Move," said Dr. Strasborg.

They ran out of the store. Andrew looked behind him. A horde of zombies ran down the street and they were catching up.

"I'm not running fast enough," said Nicholas.

"Quick," said Dr. Strasborg. "In here."

They ran into a store.

"Board the door," said Dr. Strasborg.

Andrew pushed a cabinet in front of the door.

"Good job," said Nicholas. He was out of breath.

The horde of zombies pushed against the door.

"We'll stay here for the night," said Dr. Strasborg. "We'll get the girls in the morning."

"How do you plan on passing them?" asked Andrew.

"In the morning half of them should be gone. Then we'll go through the back and take the alley."

"That won't work," said Andrew. "They'll see us."

They looked at one another.

"We need to go at night," said Nicholas.

"He's right," said Andrew.

"Okay. We go then. But I don't want to hear either of you make a sound."

They waited for nightfall. When night came the zombies were not pressed to the door. Instead they shambled around the street.

"Okay," said Dr. Strasborg. "Ready?"

"Yeah."

"Yes."

"Let's go."

He opened the back door of the store. They could barely see anything. They crossed the street into the next alleyway. There were no inhuman screams. They moved quickly but did not run. Eventually they reached the gun store. Dr. Strasborg knocked on the back door. No one answered. A zombie stood up from behind a dumpster. He ran toward them. Dr. Strasborg shot the creature in the head. Three more zombies ran to the alleyway. Andrew shot one, Dr. Strasborg shot the two others.

"Andrew?" asked Denice.

"It's us. Hurry."

The door opened and they all went in. They locked the door again.

"You made it," said Denice.

She kissed Andrew.

"Where's Kelsey?" asked Nicholas.

"She's asleep in the office room," said Denice.

She looked at Andrew.

"What happened?"

"We're fine," said Andrew. "We got caught up, but we're fine. We brought some food."

"Good," she said. "I was worried about you."

Kelsey came out of the office room.

"What happened? Where have you been?" asked Kelsey.

"We're safe now. That's all that matters," said Nicholas.

They kissed.

"I was so worried about you," said Kelsey.

They kissed again.

"We're fine," said Nicholas.

They walked into the office room kissing. Nicholas shut the door.

"Those two," said Andrew.

"Who's hungry?" asked Dr. Strasborg.

"I'll take a protein bar," said Andrew.

Denice and Andrew walked over to Dr. Strasborg, who opened one of the bags. They each grabbed a protein bar.

"Thanks," said Andrew.

"Thank you," said Denice.

They ate together.

"So what's your story?" said Denice.

"It's a long one," said Dr. Strasborg.

"Yeah?"

"I was a well-known doctor before any of this happened. I was working on the virus at a company called Merricorp."

"I knew that," said Andrew.

"What about family?" asked Denice.

"I had a daughter. God, she was just like me. She had my brain," said Dr. Strasborg. "A smaller version of me."

"What happened to them?" asked Andrew.

"They all went away. During the infection I lost them. I was working at the time. The infection was an experiment. It wasn't supposed to be like this. Somehow it got out of control."

Andrew sat back in his chair.

•

Three days passed.

"We're out of food," said Nicholas. "We need more. And protein bars and water aren't going to cut it anymore. We need canned goods."

"What we need is to find shelter in a grocery store," said Andrew.

"No. There's no way to lock a grocery store," said Dr. Strasborg. "They're too big."

"We can find a small one. A mom-and-pop place, somewhere along the coast," said Andrew.

"Well, we can't just wait here," said Nicholas.

"We need a boat. If we got a boat we could raid ports for food," said Kelsey.

"Okay, so we find a boat," said Dr. Strasborg.

"And where are we going to find keys?" said Nicholas. "They just happen to be in the boat? Or—wait—maybe we search the stores for keys. But we might as well be searching for a needle in a haystack."

"We need a place with food. We already have weapons," said Andrew.

"How about a supermarket?" asked Denice.

"We just went over this. A supermarket won't work," said Andrew.

"Okay, then. We find a corner store, one that has food," said Dr. Strasborg.

They packed the food, water and ammunition in a single bag Andrew carried. They moved in the morning, when they could see the threat coming. They went out the back door and on to the main street. The zombies slowly walked toward the survivors. If the zombies got too close they would start to run. If they started to run they would have to be shot. If they had to be shot the sound would alert more of them. The survivors moved swiftly through the streets. The ocean and port were to their right. Eventually they came across a small convenience store. They went inside.

"This is exactly what we were looking for," said Nicholas.

"Okay," said Andrew. "Let's board this place up."

"Hey, there's an upstairs—" said Denice.

A fat and old zombie fell on her from the top of the stairs. The weight crushed Denice, as the zombie took a chunk out of her neck.

"No," said Andrew.

He ran over and shot the zombie in the head. Three more zombies from upstairs tackled Andrew. The front door broke open and zombies flooded inside. Andrew shot the zombie that was on top of him.

Nicholas pointed his gun at the door and fired a few rounds. Dr. Strasborg shot and moved behind the counter beside Nicholas. Andrew looked around. Two zombies were at the bottom of the stairs. They saw him and ran toward him. Andrew fired three shots and hit both zombies in the head. They fell before him. The back door opened and more zombies pushed in. A zombie from the corner of the room crawled toward Nicholas' feet. He bit him in the leg. Nicholas screamed and shot the zombie in the head. A zombie tackled Dr. Strasborg. He shot the zombie in the head, but three more jumped on. Kelsey, who watched the back door, was overwhelmed by the horde. Nicholas had zombies from both sides running at him. He pointed the gun at his head and fired.

Three of the zombies who had run toward Nicholas turned and ran at Andrew. Andrew ran up the stairs and into a bedroom. He held his shotgun pointed at the door and waited. The first zombie ran through. He fired a shot into his head. The creature fell over. The next two monsters ran to the door and were inside the bedroom. He fired three shots and killed them both. He breathed heavily. He crawled underneath the bed and wept. Three more zombies ran into the room. They looked around. One sniffed the air. All of the sudden a boat's horn blew from the harbor. The zombies in the room left except for one. He looked out the window and saw the boat. He screamed and ran out of the room.

Andrew's hands were around his gun. The barrel was pointed at his chin. He tensed his hands. He then let go of the gun, lay his head on the hardwood floor, and sobbed. His face was red. He was a child again. He was in his house playing video games with his best friend, Laurence. They talked about girls they liked at school. Andrew lay under the bed and pulled himself out. He looked out of the window and saw hordes of zombies sprinting into the sea. Most of them flailed their arms in the water until they sank. Andrew took stock. He had five bullets left in his gun. There was food and ammo from his dead friends downstairs. But where he would go and what he would do, he wasn't sure. He looked at the boat as a glimmer of hope.

# *Coping*

S ummer is here," Bill said. He couldn't believe it was true but here it was, brighter and greener than he had ever seen it. At that moment the world changed into something magnificent and beautiful without a hint of the infection. It seemed he was dreaming. He felt as if the wind could carry him up to the sky and bring him closer to the sun.

"Where is she?" Bill wondered. "It's been 15 minutes."

"I don't know," Lewis said. "Maybe she just needs time."

"Time for what?"

"Well, this was her first time killing someone she knew. I think it hurt her." Lewis was a big black man who had been a professional bowler. He was nearing his mid-40s. "But we need to do something. Otherwise, we'll all get hurt waiting around like this."

"Ah, come on Lewis, relax. Take in the sunlight."

They were in the middle of a park.

Lewis leaned his head back on a tree. He exhaled loudly. His mind replayed the zombies he had killed. He didn't like it but he didn't much care to control his mind's images, either.

"That's more like it," Bill said. He leaned his head against a tree. He was tall, lanky, and white. He had on a long-sleeved dress shirt. He looked at his hands. "Still got these babies. That's a good sign."

"We should check on her. See if she's all right."

"All right." Bill stood up.

Lewis leaned over and picked up his 12-gauge shotgun.

"You know. I wish I didn't need this." He pumped the shotgun once.

"Yep."

Bill and Lewis walked toward the car, where Taylor had insisted she be left alone. No creatures were around. The sky suddenly grew much darker as clouds covered the sun.

"Something isn't right," said Lewis. Some evil presence could be felt but not seen. It seemed to watch him.

There was smeared ash on the ground. The air blew the smell of rotting produce through their nostrils. Fear filled their bodies and shivered their skin. Both of them had a vague uneasiness and sense that they weren't ready for what was coming for them. The quick sound of footsteps could be heard. Bill pulled out his pistol and pointed it in front of him. Lewis did the same. A zombie ran from behind a hill in front of them.

"Mine," Bill said. He aimed and fired one shot, which blasted through the creature's head. He flipped the gun around like John Wayne and sheathed his gun in the holster.

"There's more," Lewis said.

And just as he said it, a wave of zombies ran from behind the green hill in front of them. The sound echoed around the park and city. Bill and Lewis, quick to react, turned to run at the sight of the first two zombies. Bill clenched a pistol and was extremely nervous. Though he was short and not very athletic, Bill became stressed during life-or-death situations. It was stress alone, Lewis thought, that kept him alive all this time. Bill ran like a shocked gazelle.

"We're going to Pete's house," Lewis said.

Lewis thought of all the loonies he had known throughout his life. Pete had made his top three.

Before the infection, Pete Lombard had a basement filled with weapons. At work, many called him crazy though they didn't say it to his face. He was too big and too strong. He could bench-press 260 pounds and was well-trained in muay thai, wrestling, and his favorite, jeet kune do.

Pete used to work for the CIA and asked people at restaurants on more than one occasion not to announce his name. He would sometimes give a fake name instead. When Lewis asked him why, Pete gave him a short answer.

"I don't want people knowing where I am."

Lewis left it at that.

After the CIA, Pete worked for the police academy for 18 years until the infection hit. That's all he says about it. He was a bit strange and so was his intuition. But it was perhaps his intuition that led him to survive the coming of the infection. Lewis saw it like this: When a crazy thing happened, somewhere a crazy person was ready for it. He also realized that if a zombie infection could happen, so could anything else. Lewis wasn't sure how he felt about this. He didn't have time to think. They reached Pete's house.

Pete wiped the dirt off of his shoulder. He picked up the cup and brought it near his nostrils. He smelled the coffee and let out a loud and appreciative sound.

"One of the many perks for the living."

The basement was dark. Many people might wonder how he lived there but the answer was simple. If you lived during the infection, you were strong. Pete was no exception. The weak went insane. The infection made them paralyzed, sick and lazy. It made them too lazy to get food for themselves. Most of them starved in the area they holed up in, thinking about the ones they lost. The infection made you, changed you. It made your heart explode. It's a place you don't want to be and if you let it, it will kill you.

A voice from the corner of the room spoke to Pete.

"You don't like me. You want to drown me like you drown all the other creatures out there. You want to hurt me like you hurt Grandma." His voice was high-pitched. "Well, buddy, if you think I'm going to take your shit, I'll be gone by tomorrow."

"We'll see about that," Pete said.

Josh had promised to leave many times before but never did. He had lost his mind about a month ago and Pete had taken care of him since. The main reason being Pete could still see the past Josh in his eyes. Behind the mask of insanity he thought he saw a man putting it all together. He had just decided to check out is all. And when it came down to it Pete cared about Josh. He cared and Pete thought it helped his own sanity to care. It gave Pete something to do.

"I stay busy. I stay healthy," Pete said.

"Who are you talking to?" asked Lewis.

"No one. Drink your tea, man."

"Are we safe here?"

"For the time being. You guys got a place to stay besides here, though?"

"Not at the moment."

"Okay. You can stay here as long as you like."

All of the sudden there was a thud on the basement door.

"Who is it?" Pete asked.

There was no answer. A zombie broke through the door and bit Pete's neck.

"You piece of shit."

Pete took a gun from his holster and blew the shit out of the zombies' stomach until it lay on the floor. He aimed at its head and shot it between the eyes.

"Holy shit," Lewis said.

"Go!" Pete yelled. "Through the tunnel."

They ran through an area that was not known to them. They were lost. The pipe had many routes.

"What the hell is this place?" Bill asked. He was at the front of the group.

"It's a tunnel system," said Lewis.

"Shut up and move," Pete said.

Bill and Lewis ran in front of Pete and Josh. They ran down the tunnel until they needed to duck their heads to get all the way through. They saw the end of the tunnel by a ray of light. Josh helped Pete through the tunnel.

"Do you think Pete's going to be okay?" asked Bill.

"No," Lewis said.

"I hope so. We need to keep going, though."

"Oh, come off it. He's dead. You saw the bite."

"Well, I was just trying to be positive. Where to now?"

"We need to get to a house. We need food and shelter."

"Let's get into this house here."

They found a red brick house. They went through the back door. Bill walked into the kitchen. There were cooking mittens with kitten embroidery by the stove. He walked up the stairs, which were lined with family photographs. He walked into the first room he saw, with his gun pointed forward. The room was empty. He made his way back down the stairs.

"We'll stay here for the night and take shifts every three hours watching Pete and securing the house," said Bill.

"I'll take first shift," said Lewis.

"Okay. There are three bedrooms upstairs. You guys decide who gets what, but I call the master."

"You got it," said Lewis.

Josh and Bill went upstairs while Pete and Lewis sat in the living room. Lewis rested in a lazy boy while Pete lay on a sofa. He had a towel around his neck to stop the bleeding.

"So do you believe?" asked Pete.

"In what?" said Lewis.

"God."

"The only thing I believe in is the gun in my hand and my friend upstairs."

"God, you know. If that bastard doesn't let me into heaven, I'll kick his ass."

Pete coughed blood.

"I hear you."

They sat there silently for a few seconds. The city was quiet. There were no cars to be heard and there were no birds chirping. It was just them.

"Are you a religious man?" asked Lewis.

"No, but that doesn't mean I won't be praying. What about you?"

"No."

"Sometimes I think about heaven. It's been like that ever since the outbreak. I think my friends and my wife are up there waiting for me."

They sat there waiting for the sun to come up as the darkness drew over them.

# *Hunger*

The fire burned in the cabin. They covered themselves with deer hide as they huddled around the flame. The zombies haunted the woods around them.

"So, you know them?" said Bill. "Those creatures out there?"

"Yes," said Jim. "They're my family and my ex-wife's family."

"They aren't family anymore."

"That's right," said Delilah. "Those are demons, is what they are."

"I want to believe there is some way I can bring them back. They have to remember me," said Jim.

"They remember you like a wolf remembers a rabbit," said Bill.

"They're just starving," said Delilah.

Jim's stomach grumbled.

"We should do something about the windows," said Delilah. "One of them sees us in here they might jump right through it."

"They are too stupid to jump through a window," said Bill.

"Well, it doesn't take someone too smart to do it, either," said Delilah.

"All right, then. I'll get wood from the shack. Jim, you come with me," said Bill.

"Okay," said Jim.

Bill picked up his hunting rifle. They walked outside. The hut was about 50 yards from the house. Bill opened the shed door and went inside. He found wood planks and handed a stack to Jim. They walked back to the hut. Before they made it to the cabin a scream echoed through the trees. They stood still for a few seconds. When nothing happened they walked back to the cabin.

"I brought a hammer," said Jim. He laid the hammer on the table. "And nails."

"Let's get to it," said Bill.

They boarded up the windows and went back to the fire.

"Why don't we leave this place?" asked Delilah. "There is nothing here but the undead."

"You think it's bad here? You got another thing coming thinking it'll be any better in the city or anywhere else," said Jim.

"I guess you're right," said Delilah. "Why don't you two go hunting for food?"

"Well, let's go and catch something, Jim," said Bill.

"Okay," said Jim.

Bill picked up his hunting rifle. The two of them left the cabin. Delilah locked the door behind them. They searched for small game such as squirrels or rabbits. If they were really lucky they would spot a deer. Jim held his gun close to him. They both crouched. Jim followed Bill's lead.

"Shh," said Bill.

They heard a rustle behind them.

Bill turned his gun. There was another rustle behind them. Bill turned his gun again. Jim imagined a woman laughing in the woods. Her voice echoed through the trees. A squirrel dashed past them. Bill fired his rifle without really aiming.

"Shit," said Bill. They went back to the hut unsuccessful in their hunt.

"Yay, you made it back okay," said Delilah.

"We did but we didn't find anything," said Jim. He walked over to the bookshelf. "What's this book?" He picked up the book. "*Pre-Socratic Philosophers*, huh?"

"That's from my nephew, Stone. He majored in philosophy. A real bookworm. Like I'd ever read something like that. But, you know, with kids you just need to pretend you like their gift," said Bill.

Delilah and Bill watched the fire while Jim read the book. An hour passed by.

"This philosopher Zeno said there is no movement. For example, think of a runner who needs to get to the finish line. He first needs to cross the midway point and then the midway point of that and then the midway point of that, to infinity. Someone can't walk a distance of infinity when they have a finite amount of time, so the runner never really moves. Isn't that interesting?" said Jim.

"Don't read too much into it, Jim. It's stupid, is what it is," said Bill.

"But that would mean my wife is out there not moving and that I could find her. And she wouldn't hurt me. Maybe I could make her normal again," said Jim.

"Boy, you talking crazy," said Bill. "Just sick in the mind. Even if you do believe this Zeno fellow. The philosophy works both ways. You and her couldn't move from where you are."

Jim heard the scream again. Jim unlocked and opened the door. He went out into the wilderness.

"Now, boy, don't be stupid," said Bill. He stood at the door.

Jim ran through the trees. He eventually came to the cliff where his wedding was. Chairs were thrown to the ground. Tables were overturned. The cake rotted in the moonlight. And there she was, standing near the cliff where the sermon had taken place. She looked at the moon almost as if she were searching for something within herself. Jim walked up to her.

"Where have you been?" he asked.

She turned around and a tear fell from her face. She stood there motionless. He took her hand and she held his. They looked at the moon together. For a second everything was perfect, but she suddenly started to jerk back and forth, as if she were having a seizure. Her eyes rolled to the back of her head and she fell to the ground.

"Sylvia," said Jim. "Sylvia."

The shaking stopped and her eyes were closed. They opened and she did not recognize Jim. Whatever was human about her had been drowned out by the infection. She screamed and tried to bite him. He started to cry as he held her down by her arms. He picked her up and pushed her off the side of the cliff. When he got back to the cabin Bill opened the door.

"Come in."

The fire was out and Jim got under the deerskin blanket on the floor. He lay his head down on the pillow and tried to fall asleep. He woke up in the morning to Bill placing wood in the fireplace.

"Well," said Bill. "We got ourselves a problem. We haven't eaten for four days and my wife is getting hungry. There isn't any food we can catch."

Jim looked for the gun. It was on the dresser.

"Now, I don't like it any more than you do but we need to thin—" said Bill.

The gun cocked. Bill turned around.

"What the hell are you doing, boy?" asked Bill.

"What's your plan?" said Jim.

"I don't know. I just wanted to talk about it, is all. We got no food here and Delilah has been complaining. Maybe we could cut off your leg or something," said Bill.

"Maybe we could cut off yours," said Jim.

"I'm your only hunter," said Bill.

"Not very good at it though, are you? I could hunt just fine. So let's see it, Bill. Cut off your leg," said Jim.

"All right," said Bill. "Maybe I wasn't thinking straight. Just put down the gun and we'll think of something else."

Jim put the gun back on the dresser.

"We need a new food supply," said Jim.

"How about the zombies? Aren't they meat? We could try and eat them," said Bill.

"We could, but the meat is rotten. We'd get sick," said Jim.

"Not if you boil it long enough you won't," said Bill.

"What other options do we have?" said Delilah. "Best idea I've heard from the two of you all day."

"All right, it's settled then. We kill one of them creatures—" said Bill.

"Demons," said Delilah.

"Right," said Bill. "We kill one of them demons and have it for lunch."

Bill and Jim walked out the front door.

"Hey, you blood-sucking cocksucking faggots. I'm calling you," said Bill.

There was silence in the woods. They couldn't see anyone in front of them.

"Well," said Bill. "We better get moving."

They walked over a small hill and found what they were looking for. A zombie walking into a tree.

"Hey you," said Bill. "Your whore of a mother told me to do something to you."

The zombie looked at them and then showed its teeth. It started to walk toward them. Bill took aim and fired. The bullet went through the front of the zombie's skull and out the back. Bill and Jim dragged the creature back to their cabin.

"I got a machete in the shack. I'll be right back," said Bill.

The zombie's skin was gray. Bill came back with a machete and chopped off its thigh. He then put it over the fireplace to cook.

"Oooh, boy. This is the smartest I ever been," said Bill. "We got food here for a week."

He let the meat cook for an hour over the fire and then cut it into small pieces. They all ate a piece of the thigh.

"Well, it might not be much, but it's food." Said Bill.

"Yep," said Jim. "I can't taste anything. It's charred."

"Quit your bellyaching," said Delilah.

An hour after they all felt sick.

"You said it was fine to eat," said Jim.

"I thought it was," said Bill. "Clearly, I'm not an expert. I was wrong."

They threw up and had diarrhea. Jim's eyes were closing and opening. His skin was white. In the next two days Bill and Delilah had recovered but Jim was still ill. He looked skinnier because of the lack of food, the sweating, and the constant vomiting. On day three Jim died.

"Well, darling. I hate to say it—" said Bill.

"But here's breakfast, lunch and dinner," said Delilah.

# *Origins*

T he lights were out but there were flames from the stove. They provided the only light besides the moon and the stars that penetrated the windows of the house.

Outside, Michael Dorn moved in semi-darkness. He looked up and saw no clouds in the sky. He knew there were better nights to move, but he could not pick and choose. He needed food. His wet combat boots stepped on the cold grass. He stopped before a sign that read "Welcome to" on its top half. On the bottom half of the sign, was "Bedford" spelled out with big bold letters. The sign was painted farm colors of yellow, red and orange. The sign looked new, clean and without bullet holes.

He looked past the sign and saw houses. They were white and two stories high with gray roofs. The lawns at the front of the houses were dark green and well-groomed. The cars were also parked on designated parking spots and were not scattered around the street with broken windows. Michael shook his head.

*I must be dead*, he thought. He looked at the town with his mouth slightly open. "I hope there's food here," he said. He took a heavy breath of cold air.

He had traveled through towns, lakes and cities. The few towns he visited were small and untouched. The lake he visited contained no life but had a dam at the end, and the city he visited contained rusted cars losing their paint, and skyscrapers that were dirty and tall. The corpses at the lake had forgotten how to swim. They flailed their arms in the water as they sunk to the bottom. The city was the most dangerous because of its high population of undead. The cars were still on the sidewalks and streets. Many streets and sidewalks were completely blocked with cars and made travel difficult and sometimes impossible. Shops' display windows and door windows were oftentimes broken. Skyscrapers accumulated dirt and trash even though their sturdiness remained.

Michael moved to the city of Las Vegas but he had grown up in a gated community that was similar to the one before him. He walked to the first house on the right side of the street, drew his pistol from the holster, and went into the house's backyard. He moved to the back door and carefully turned the doorknob. As he tried to walk silently through the house, his boots still made a low-toned and low-volume echo.

*Okay, this is just like Iraq. They can hear you but you can't hear them. They can see you but you can't see them.* He served in the Army for several years, finishing a year before the infection broke out. During that interim he got engaged to his high school girlfriend. Michael had forgotten her name. "Almost done here," he said quietly. He had circled the house with his pistol and he walked toward the kitchen.

His vision blurred and he swayed back and forth. He paid close attention to the sounds around him. He walked past the front door and noticed the room had stairs that led up to the second floor. He moved to the dining room. Two large windows looked out at the yard. The shades were up and the blue light from the moon and stars shone on the hardwood floor, china cabinet, wooden table and wooden chairs. He walked past the dining room and into the kitchen.

He took a pan from above the stove and placed it over the fire. He looked into the cabinet above the pans and found cooking oil.

*It's a miracle,* he thought with a tired brain and unfilled stomach. He looked through his bag and sifted to the bottom. He picked up a can of beans and looked around in the drawers. He found a knife and stabbed the metal lid of the beans. Once the can opened, he poured the beans into the pan and sat on a tall stool. The beans seared and Mike looked out the window behind him. It looked quiet and cold outside as he saw silhouettes of the houses around the block. Multiple two-story houses lined up against one another.

*Just a flicker of light from one of these houses, please,* he thought.

For two years, he was without a friend. The street was clear except for cars parked on the side of the street or in their garages. He wondered why the cars were still on the street and why the gas was still on. The other places he had been were trashed with mostly garbage, debris, cars and bodies. It reminded him of an impenetrable bubble during the apocalypse.

He turned off the stove and grabbed a towel above it. He then grabbed a fork from one of the drawers. There was the sound of a twig snapping near the window. The sprinklers on the lawns turned on. Mike turned around and looked at the window. He held his pistol in his left hand, took the meal into the dark living room, and set them on a table. He sat on a couch and looked around the room. There was a television in front of him and one window on either side of it. There was a leather recliner against the left wall of his vision. A circular knitted design of red, white and blue lay on the recliner. He looked up and saw a small brass chandelier hanging from the center of the ceiling.

After these visuals his mind kicked in again. He looked at his beans and scooped them quickly into his mouth, both out of hunger and fear of the sound. He finished his meal and picked up his backpack at the front door. He walked to the back of the house where he heard a sound from the basement. It was a loud thump. He put down his backpack quickly and quietly, pulled out his gun from one of its pockets, and clung with his back to the wall. He stopped at the door between kitchen and living room.

*Shit,* he thought. *Why didn't I think to look there?*

He opened the door and held his pistol steady down the stairs. The room was pitch black. He flipped the light switch to the right of him, but the lights did not turn on. He went back to his backpack and grabbed a flashlight from his bag. He returned to the stairs and turned on his flashlight before he quickly closed the door behind him.

The room seemed normal and empty. There were laundry machines to his right with a small pile of red and blue towels on top. There was dust made visible by the lights. There was a small window in the room and the moon shone through it, light blue and gray. There was a low hum that could be heard throughout and a creak upstairs. Mike turned his gun around and pointed it up the stairs. He backed down the stairs and turned his gun to the laundry machine. He looked for the source of the hum but noticed the machine was off. He bent down to the concrete floor. The sound of the hum increased. He heard classical music play below him. He looked up at the door and saw it was open. A shadow watched him from upstairs then moved out of sight. Mike pointed his gun at the door and walked up the stairs. He turned right into the kitchen.

"Who's there?"

He heard a noise in the other room. He walked past the kitchen and into the dining room. The silhouette of a woman sat at the table. All was black except for the portions covered by the moon coming through the windows behind the woman. The area around her was light blue but she was still black. He sat down on a chair across from her.

"What do you want with me?" he asked.

"I've been following you for some time."

"How long?"

"The infection started two years ago. That's when. You already know, Dan."

He flinched.

"My name is not Dan, it's Mike. Looks like you haven't done your paperwork."

"Come on, Dan. You know me. Don't you?"

She moved forward in the moonlight. Her face was beautiful and soft. She had dark blonde hair that fell a few inches past her collarbone. She lifted her hand to touch his face.

"Don't touch me!"

He flew backward off the chair. He got up and pointed his gun but no one was there.

"Come on, Dan. Don't you remember?"

"Go away! I don't. I don't know!"

He backed into a corner.

"I don't remember." He slid down the wall to a crouched position.

"Don't you remember me?" The voice came from the kitchen.

He looked at the kitchen from where he sat.

"Go away! Don't...don't come any closer. I have a gun! What the hell is this?"

A woman crawled into view. Her hair was sparse on her head. Her face was hidden from view. She wore a tattered white shirt. Her arms were covered with dried dirt. The woman started to cry as she inched her way toward him. Her legs were motionless.

Dan shot her. The darkness covered the motionless body.

"Don't you remember?" Her voice was high-pitched.

She crawled toward him once again and she moved into the blue light of the moon and stars. First her head was illuminated. She looked at him. Her face had a hole in her right cheek, her eyes were light blue and blind, and her jaw was open wide. Her skin looked dirty, old and dry like leather. Dan fired another shot at her face but the bullet did not pierce her skin.

"I'm sorry," he said. "I tried to meet you but I couldn't make it."

She was 15 feet in front of him.

"I was getting ready," he said. He looked up at the ceiling. His eyes watered. "I didn't know this would happen to you. Okay? I went to the restaurant but you weren't there."

"You didn't go," she said. Her voice echoed through the room and his mind.

"I've regretted that decision to this day. What if I had been there? I'm sorry but I can't change the past."

He looked at her. Her mouth was open and she lay her head on the floor.

"Goodbye, Dan."

"Goodbye, Tricia. I'm sorry I forgot. I'm sorry." He bent down to the floor and cried.

The dead body remained motionless on the floor when the sound of broken glass could be heard from another room. Zombies surrounded the house. Dan looked out the window and saw them walking toward him as they spread out across the neighborhood.

Dan took a chair and broke one of the windows that looked out on the front yard. He ran through the kitchen and grabbed any food he could find. He also filled up a canteen of water. He ran back to the dining room and jumped through the hole, with his backpack on his back, and his pistol in his hand. The zombies were within reach but could not keep up with Dan. He ran into the dark forest as they shambled toward him.

# Is Anybody Out There?

K yle looked around him. There were cans on his floor, on the kitchen counters, and on his table. He lay in his bed. His shirt was off and so were his pants. He wore striped red boxers. A few minutes ago he finished his last can of tomato soup. He was out of food. His girlfriend, Kaylie, was in the other room staring out the window. It was summer time and the apartment was very warm.

"We need to get food," said Kyle.

It had been two years since the start of the infection.

"Okay," she said.

They walked to his apartment's front door. He moved the chair that leaned under the doorknob.

"Oh," he said. "Almost forgot."

He walked over to his kitchen and picked up a lead pipe and a katana.

"One for you and one for me," he said.

He handed the samurai sword to Kaylie and opened the door. They walked into the hallway slowly and looked both ways. The walls were white. In front of him was a blood stain of a hand smeared along the wall. All the doors were broken into from past food raids. They walked up the stairs and reached the top floor of the building. They went to the first door, which was locked. Kyle kicked down the door. A zombie lunged for him. He took his pipe and beat the creature over the head. They went into the apartment's kitchen. He opened the cupboards but found nothing except one can of vegetable beef soup. Kyle put the can in his bag.

They went back to the hallway and tried the next door. It was locked. He kicked the door down. Kaylie walked in the room. The apartment was spotless.

"Whoever was here took good care of the place," said Kyle.

"I'm sure they tried," said Kaylie. "They figured if they let this place go, their sanity goes with it."

They sat down on a couch.

"Is there any food?" asked Kaylie.

Kyle got up and went to the kitchen.

"No."

Kyle walked to the door.

"We could go to the landlord's apartment," said Kaylie. "I always wonder what happened to him."

"I don't know," said Kyle. "Maybe he went to the city, which has been fended off with a wall built around it."

"Can we go?"

"Anyone with a beating heart can go."

Kyle saw a radio on the living room table and decided to switch it on.

"All survivors of the plague should come to Paterson, New Jersey. We have food and shelter here."

Kaylie switched off the radio.

"That's about a two-hour drive," said Kyle. "That's not far at all."

"The freeway isn't drivable in some parts. We'd have to take the surface streets, which could be very dangerous."

"Our car is still intact in the garage, so we can make the drive. All right, I know the way. And the reward outweighs the risk, as we may finally get to sleep with some peace and quiet."

They went to the landlord's apartment and stocked up on food. They took all the belongings they could carry and put them in Kyle's apartment.

"We'll need to wait till daylight," said Kyle, "so we can see what's in the garage."

"I'm not going to be able to sleep," said Kaylie.

"Suit yourself."

He walked into the bedroom and closed the door. Kaylie walked over to the drapes and pulled them up, but the moon could not be seen.

Kaylie woke up slowly with the sun on her face. She leaned forward and looked at her kitchen. Kyle ate canned corn.

"Here, have some."

He handed Kaylie his corn and when she finished they left the apartment. They walked down the stairs and into the garage. The sun lit the area from the garage's opening. They got into Kyle's car and drove out. The streets were littered with the walking dead. Abandoned cars blocked the road and some were on the sidewalks. A red sedan hit a light pole. Kyle swerved around abandoned cars and looked for the freeway entrance. He turned onto the freeway as he passed a creature who was gray, bald and lacked a jaw. The freeway looked the same as the streets. Cars were abandoned. They passed a blue sedan with an undead trapped inside. He banged on the windshield when he saw the survivors pass.

They eventually made it to New Jersey after five hours of driving. The city of Paterson was less populated than New York. The freeway carved a path to their destination through forests and meadows. When they reached the city they found nothing.

"What happened? I thought it said—" said Kyle.

"The radio said there was a town here. It's on 89.9 FM."

Kyle turned the radio to 89.9 FM.

"All survivors of the plague should come to Paterson, New Jersey. We have food and shelter here," said the voice.

"See," said Kaylie.

"Shh," said Kyle.

"All survivors of the plague should come to Paterson, New Jersey. We have food and shelter here," said the voice again.

"You idiot," said Kyle. "It's a repeat. Who knows how long it was before they were killed off?"

"Well, how was I supposed to know they were killed off?"

Kyle let out a sigh and put his head on the steering wheel.

"Our tank is half full. We have only 150 to 200 miles left," said Kyle.

"Check the other radio stations. Maybe they moved or there is somewhere else we can go."

Kyle went one by one up the station list. There was nothing but static until they reached 89.3 FM.

"We are students of Trinity College who have holed up in Lone Mountain. We have the area secure. If you want to join us, yell at us from below. We will activate the elevators if we see you are not a threat."

"There," said Kaylie. "I knew we'd find something."

"Let's not get our hopes up. If it's anything like the last radio message, they're already dead."

They drove to Hartford, Connecticut. Prior to the zombie apocalypse, Hartford had the highest crime rate in the country in ratio to the surface area of the city. Not much had changed since the apocalypse. Buildings were still crumbling. The houses were old, small and made of brick. They reached Trinity College and parked in a lot at the front of the campus.

"I know where Lone Mountain is," said Kaylie.

"I have an idea as well."

He looked at the tallest building on campus. They drove to the building. There was an elevator on the first floor. They got out of the car with weapons in hand.

"Hey," said Kyle.

Kyle banged his pipe on the metal door. Someone looked out the window. The elevator moved down but the noise attracted unwelcome guests. Three zombies ran at them. Two were shot down and the other had his head bashed in by a lead pipe. The elevator reached the bottom. The doors opened and a brown-haired student beckoned them in. The student had big eyebrows, short hair and a chiseled face. The elevator went up.

"Where are you from?" asked the student.

"First off, what's your name?" said Kyle.

"My name is Stone. That's one hell of a way to treat someone who has saved you."

"Sorry," said Kyle. "It's been a while since we've been around other people."

"Don't mention it," said Stone.

"Well, we are very grateful," said Kaylie.

"You're safe now. We've got the place fortified, with tons of food," said Stone.

"We could have killed you, you know," said Kyle.

"You don't seem like the killing type," said Stone.

The elevator reached the top. They all stepped out and surveyed their surroundings. There was another brown-haired boy who was a little shorter than Stone.

"This is my brother Bradford," said Stone.

"Nice to meet you," said Bradford.

"This is Farrington," Stone said.

Farrington leaned on the wall and stared at the visitors. He had buzzed blond hair.

"Pleasure to meet you," said Farrington.

"This is my girlfriend, Leah," said Stone.

She had big eyes, long wavy brown hair and big lips.

"We've been here since the start of the infection," said Stone.

"How did you survive?" asked Kyle.

"There are three entrances to this floor," said Stone. "One is connected to the other building. That's the main open hallway, and it's pretty big. There's a door at the end of the hallway and it's usually locked with a key-card system. Since we are running on generators the locks don't work. We blocked the hallway with mattresses. The next entrance is the stairway from the bottom of the building. We blocked that with the metal springs underneath the mattresses. That was hard. Well, actually, all of it was difficult. Finally, the generator can be turned on there, in that room. You pull the lever and activate the elevator."

# Picking Up Pieces of Glass

Andrew woke up in a cardboard box. He was in a newly fortified city—a safe zone. He smelled of urine. His hair was matted and he had an unkempt beard. He stood up and walked to the end of the alley. Police cars drove past him on the street.

"What's that all about?" asked Mike.

"I don't know," said Andrew. He turned around and looked up at the skyscrapers. Their windows gleamed.

"You think we'll ever live in a skyscraper?" asked Mike.

"One day," said Andrew. "If we're lucky."

"Come on, let's eat."

Most of the stores they passed had their doors and windows boarded. When they reached their destination, they saw a line of people out the door. They were all dressed in rags and filthy clothes. Their hair was matted. Mike and Andrew walked to the back of the line. When they reached the front they were served chili.

"Thanks," said Andrew.

"No problem."

Andrew and Mike sat down on one of the many benches.

"So when did you get to the city?" asked Mike.

"I got here ten days ago," said Andrew. "How about you?"

"Oh, I've been here for as long as I can remember."

"Who stays in the skyscrapers?"

"The politicians and the Army generals. There are also some rich people who have international connections to get food and supplies. They live up there, too."

"I thought the world was hit by the infection. Or was it just the U.S.?"

"You're right, kind of. The world did get infected but some countries handled the infection better than others. North Korea, for example, went on full lock-down. The infected had a hard time crossing the border because of the intense military presence and the harsh mountain terrain."

"Oh," said Andrew. "Who told you all of this?"

"A buddy," said Mike. "From my understanding, we're winning the war. In the beginning it was chaos and a lot of people died. I heard over 4 billion perished but there were places that survived. Places like this. The military bases were easily defended and eventually expanded their borders to include this city."

"Do you think we could join the military? We could take baths and get clothes that way."

"They don't allow people to join anymore. They don't have enough room for us."

"Sucks to be us."

They finished their chili and walked out of the soup kitchen. Some looked at Andrew with curiosity as he left. They walked next to the giant wall that blocked off the city and after a few minutes came to stairs. They walked up and had a view over the wall.

"Isn't that something?" said Andrew.

"It is."

"What did you do before the infection?"

"I was in the Marines for a while. Then I gave that up for a normal life. My family doesn't know I was a Marine. They'd kill me if they heard. But while I was a civilian the infection hit. It took over my town, my children, my wife, until finally it was only me and my dog. He was the best dog. He always knew when danger was around, so I kept him as long as I could. And then one day he was just gone. I don't know what happened to him. He just vanished. What about you? How'd you get here?"

"I came from a long ways away. We were stuck in a town by the sea. I don't know how we got out. Well, we actually didn't make it out. I did and they died. My friends. One of them was a guy named Nick. At least I think that's what his name was. He had a funny way of making you laugh. The smartest guy I knew. He found out what the infection was. I don't know what all of this is for. I mean, this is no way of life. Sure, I get food, shelter and medicine, but what else? I don't know, maybe I'm complaining too much."

"No, no you're doing fine. You're right. This is a shithole, but it works and we need to make the best of it. Look up and remember: Things always get better. The more we win this war the more likely we'll have a better life. As time goes on, maybe we'll have homes to live in."

"You have some imagination. You know, I used to be a big football star. I remember the lights and fans and the glory. I remember it all. The girls were easy to come by, too. We'd all party at my friend's house because his parents didn't care if we got drunk. Yep. Those were the times." He lay down on the ground and looked up at the sky. "I can remember some things before the infection, but usually I see my friends getting killed by those things. I don't know what to do."

"You can talk to yourself," said Mike.

"What do you mean?" asked Andrew.

"I mean you can talk to me."

"Yeah, well. I guess it ain't much, but what's a doctor cost around here? A doctor can't fix me anyways."

"You keep thinking that and it'll come true."

"It is true. The things I've seen, no one should have to go through. Not ever. I thought there was a God, but not anymore. Not after this. When I was rich. Well, not rich, but living well. When things were okay. You know? When I wasn't poor and on the streets. All of it was too good to be true. And then it all went away, like a flash. It all seems so distant now, like it never happened. I guess that's how I cope with things. You get as far away from something horrible as you can. And keep it at bay like that. You know, like America used to do to those African kids. We just stood by and did nothing. We just watched. But now I know why. I know what it's like to face that. To face death and murder. Things I should never have seen. I know what it's like. I don't know how to live a normal life anymore. I don't know what normal is after this."

"There's always something good around the corner."

Andrew looked over at Mike.

"I had this girl before and during the infection. Her name was Denice. I always had to tell her what to do. She just froze in fear. The first time it happened, she was as useless as a pet rock. I think the first time the infection hit I actually had to carry her to the school building so she wouldn't get eaten." Andrew laughed.

"You care about people and put them before yourself."

"I guess I do. I guess it isn't so bad. When you put it into words like that, the infection can be a pretty funny thing. Like a clean slate from all the suburban shit we grew up with. Something new. I mean, yeah, it was terrible. But some good came from it, too. We're free now. Free to do whatever we want. Sleep during the day. Walk around at night."

"Shit, I got this lice on me, though. That isn't fun."

"No, it isn't. I think I'm going insane."

"Are you? I wouldn't know it, anyways. So there's no use in trying to know, is there?"

"I guess not. Well, that's just great. What good you did for me. Thanks for the help."

"Look, I'm not a doctor. I was just trying to help. If you weren't my only friend, I'd punch you in the face right now. You know you're insane, don't you?"

"Get away from me."

Mike vanished. Andrew just stood there and then walked off. He passed people who were dressed like him. People who had the same matted clothing. One man had on a dirty black bowler. Andrew walked into a bar.

"Sorry, kid. We don't serve underage drinkers here," said the bartender. He was fat and had on a white tank-top with brown stains on it. He was also bald except on the side of his head, which had brown hair. He had big eyes and big lips.

"I'm just here to see somebody," said Andrew.

"Oh, yeah. Who might that be?"

"Her."

He pointed to a blonde woman in the corner of the bar. She had a 1920s short-hair bob. He walked over to her and grabbed her by the shoulders.

"Baby, I missed you so much," he said.

"What the hell. Get off me, you creep. I don't know you," said the woman.

"I'm sorry I ever left you, baby. The infected won't get to you again."

"What are you, crazy?" said the woman. She was standing with her back against the bar. "Get away from me."

"All right, that's enough," said the bartender.

He walked over to Andrew and threw him out.

# No More Running

The Army rescued Pete a few months ago. They cured him from the infection. Soon after being cured Pete volunteered to go on food raids. He was trained to extract food, medicine, water and other essential items. Lewis and Josh had signed up, too. The zombie horde had diminished. Their corpses rotted away as their food supply became scarce. But even as the zombie threat lessened, Pete thought his death was imminent.

*They are the most frightening things I have ever encountered*, thought Pete. *I used to think it was scary being an officer of the law, but I had it easy. I can't stop, though. Not until my job is done.*

Josh was unconscious and lay on the floor. Pete dragged him by his shoulders.

"Goddamn it, Josh, wake up. Shit hit the fan. Come on, man."

Lewis grabbed Josh's legs. Pete and Lewis lifted Josh up and carried him to the backyard.

"Hurry up," said Pete.

"Okay, okay," said Lewis.

Pete opened the back door and they walked down the patio steps. Leafless bushes surrounded the backyard. A brown fence ran behind the bushes. At the back of the fence was a wooden gate. The yard was absent of immediate danger. The sun shone on their faces. Pete looked at the sky with squinted eyes. He opened the back gate. They moved Andrew behind the fence, and then rested their heads. The zombies trying to get inside the house had made it through. They ran through the back door looking for their meal but saw no one. One zombie with wilted cheeks screamed in the air. Josh opened his eyes.

"What happened?" Josh asked.

Pete put his finger to his lips and pointed at the fence. Lewis kept his back to the fence. They were far from the extraction point. The helicopter would depart with or without them in 45 minutes. There was no way of making it without being spotted.

"Fuck it," Lewis said. "We got to stand and fight. We don't have time."

"No more running?" Pete asked him.

"No more running," he replied.

"You know," Pete said. "If Lewis keeps looking like a damn zombie maybe they'll run right past him and go straight for us."

"That's not funny," said Lewis.

Pete cackled loudly at this and Lewis and Josh followed suit. Their bodies filled with energy and they felt invincible. Their laughter came from their stomachs. It was deep and soulful. They all knew there was no other way to get out of there. They had to fight through to get to the extraction point.

"You know," Josh said. "We're really going to do this?"

"It's the only way," Lewis said.

Pete and Josh looked at him. They could live off the food they found in the neighborhood, but for how long? They could maybe find a functioning car, if there weren't so many zombies.

Josh crouched at the back gate. Pete kicked down a part of the fence. Josh sighed.

"He's always got to be the flashy one," said Josh.

One of the two zombies on the lawn screamed. Pete shot the zombie in the head.

"First!" Pete yelled.

"One down," Lewis said.

*A hundred million to go,* Pete thought.

Three more zombies ran at them. All were taken down, but they got halfway across the yard and 15 feet from their intended victims. What came next was a wave of zombies. They ran like a thick snake through the doorway of the house.

*This is it,* Pete thought. "I love you guys so much."

"See you in hell!" yelled Lewis.

"Not me!" Pete yelled.

Pete's finger pulled quickly. He shot 13 shots with his pistol and got in another magazine before the zombies had reached Josh.

"How do you like this?" Josh asked.

He pulled a grenade from his pocket and pulled the pin.

Pete and Lewis ran away from Josh. Neither of them knew he had a grenade. The grenade went off and took the lives of the zombies crowded around. Pete shot the rest of the zombies one by one and refilled the magazine. His pockets were empty.

"Last mag," Pete said.

Lewis ran out of bullets. He kicked the first zombie that ran toward him. The zombie's feet flew toward the sky and Lewis felt his boot step through the zombie's stomach. The next zombie came from the left of the zombie on the ground. Lewis threw his large fist at the zombie's face. The skull of the creature shattered. Another zombie tackled Lewis. More zombies surrounded him. They ripped Lewis apart, piece by piece.

Pete reloaded his weapon. A zombie reached him. He ducked and the zombie flew over his back. He shot it in the face when it was on the ground. Another zombie ran toward him as Pete shot the first zombie on the ground. The zombie tackled Pete. He took his gun and shot the zombie from underneath the chin. Pete got up quickly and saw three zombies no more than six feet away from him. He fired his pistol three times. All three of the zombies fell. He had six bullets left. There were 12 zombies running toward him. He fired six shots. Five out of the six hit the heads of the zombies. He ran toward the sixth and punched in his skull. More of the creatures had come from around the neighborhood after hearing gunshots. One tackled Pete. The creature ate his flesh. Pete looked at the sky. He felt no pain. His body was numb. Pete lost consciousness after he looked at the bright yellow sun, vivid blue sky and white clouds.

# Demons

The cabin door opened. Two men walked in, brandishing weapons.

"Who the hell are you?" asked Bill.

Delilah lay behind him.

"We've come to rescue you," said the first man. "We're taking you to a city outside Los Angeles known as Free City. It's safe there."

Another man walked in. They all had on black military attire. The one in the middle had blond hair and a crew cut. The man to his right was bald. The man to his left had dreadlocks.

"Now, wait just a moment," said Bill. "We don't want to go anywhere."

"Let me introduce you to my compadres," said the blond one. "I'm Max. This is Philip to my left and Carl to my right. Now you can either go easy or go hard. There's a new ordinance in our city that we pick up survivors like you. We need you to help run the place."

"Well, we ain't leaving," said Bill.

"Looks like they want it the hard way, boys. Grab the girl," said Max.

The two men grabbed Delilah pushed her against the wall of the cabin. She cried. Carl unzipped his pants and started to unzip her jeans.

"No," said Delilah.

"Okay already, we'll go with you peacefully," said Bill.

"Oh, you mean this?" asked Max. "We were going to do this anyways."

●

Bill and Delilah sat near the bow of the warship.

"Here's some bread and water," said Max. "Think of us as your saviors."

He walked away. Within a week's time they reached Free City. The city is laid in ruin. Sheet metal is used to construct watchtowers. Everything is rusted and people wear tattered clothes. The ground is muddy.

"Well, here we are," said Max.

Delilah and Bill followed Max.

"You're going to be what some would call slaves," said Max. "You work for food. That's it. There's no sense in trying to bring justice here. A band of mercenaries run this operation and we will shoot you on sight if you start trouble. Right here is where you can get your haircut, if you have money."

They walked a little further.

"Here is the bar," said Max. "There's your slave house down the road. It's not pretty when it rains but other than that it should be fine. Because I like your woman so much I'll give you 50 bucks. You can spend it however you like. Here's your house. Work starts at eight so show up outside in the morning."

He walked off.

"Let's go to the bar," said Bill.

They walked into the pub. It was pretty much empty except for a few military personnel in the corner making a lot of noise. Delilah and Bill took the booth farthest away from them.

"We have to get out of here," said Delilah.

"I know. I know. But how?" asked Bill.

"We need to leave before they realize we're slaves. Right now we just look like common folk," said Delilah.

"Okay," said Bill. "Let's go."

They walked out of the bar and made for the entrance of the city. As they walked past the entrance they expected to hear someone shout at them. That never happened, so they continued walking. They followed the road until it was night. They set up camp in the forest beside the road. A car pulled up and stopped near where they were. A spotlight was attached to the back of the car. The car stopped in front of two men who were walking along the road.

"Hey," said the man in the car. "We're looking for some prisoners. They seemed to have escaped. You see anyone walk past you?"

"No," said the pedestrian. "We haven't seen anyone."

"Okay, then," said the man in the car. He drove up the road and out of sight.

"Shoot, they call it Free City," said Bill. "What a joke."

"Where are we heading?" asked Delilah.

"Somewhere away from here. We'll head up the road and see if a city or refuge is there."

"That's a shit idea."

"You got a better plan?"

"No, but it's still a shit idea."

Bill and Delilah eventually reached Los Angeles.

"We need to go somewhere safe."

"What's that you got in your hand?"

"It's a star map. Shows you where the celebrities live."

"Gimme that. The Playboy Mansion. Ain't no place safer than that. They probably got security guards and tons of hot women lounging around the pool. Hell, we may even meet Hugh Hefner. What do you think about that?"

"I think it sounds nice if you're a man."

"It's safe. They probably got gates to keep out all the creatures."

"Demons."

"That's what I said. All the demons."

"Okay, then. If you think it best."

They walked a few blocks until they reached the front gate. They crawled under the gate and walked up the driveway. There was a hill to the left of them where the grass was brown. They walked up to the front of the house. The fountain at the center of the driveway was turned off. Everything else seemed normal. There were no windows broken or any sign of burglary.

"Why ain't anyone stole from this place yet?" asked Delilah.

"Nothing to steal but food and water," said Bill. "People probably took what they could from their own homes and left the city."

"Where are all them creatures? I haven't seen too many of them since we arrived."

"They're dying off like they were back home. Who knows why."

"Jesus, Bill. That's why. Jesus couldn't let us suffer like this for much longer."

"Maybe you're right."

"I am right."

"That's what I said. You're right."

"Let's go inside and see if we can find some food and water."

"I was expecting a more friendly atmosphere."

Delilah slapped the back of his head.

"And what's that supposed to mean?" asked Delilah.

"You know, like naked chicks," said Bill.

She slapped the back of his head again.

"You know, Bill, sometimes I think you have dung for brains."

They walked to the front door. It was locked. They walked around the house.

"One of these doors got to open," said Bill. "How else did everyone leave?"

They went to the side door, where the cooks and butlers watched television on their breaks. They tried the door and it was open.

"See?" said Bill.

"Hush," said Delilah.

They walked in and turned right. They were in the kitchen. They checked all the cupboards but nothing was there. They went into the butlers' pantry. They checked the refrigerator, but that too was empty.

"Dang it," said Bill. "Ain't nothing here to eat or drink."

"Let's keep looking, honey," said Delilah.

They went through the living room and into the great hall. A giant chandelier hung over the white marble floors.

"Maybe in there," said Delilah.

She pointed to the movie room. They walked in and heard something peculiar. They heard voices but didn't know from where. Bill put his finger to his mouth. They moved quietly until the voices were louder. They were coming from inside the wall.

*There must be a switch*, thought Bill. Bill felt around the walls for a lever or something, until he gave up. He sat down against the wall and his head hit the back of a button. A loud buzz was heard and he fell backward as a secret door opened.

"Who's there?" said a voice.

"It's just me and my wife," said Bill. "We're looking for food and water."

A man walked up the stairs pointing a gun. He aimed it at Delilah and Bill.

"There's no need for that. If you want us to leave, we'll leave," said Bill.

Another voice called from below.

"Make sure they're not armed and let them in," the voice said.

"Yes sir," said the security guard. He pointed his gun upstairs. "Move."

Bill and Delilah walked up the stairs. They were searched.

"They're clear," said the security guard.

"Bring them down," said the voice.

They walked down the stairs and saw Hugh Hefner and Crystal Hefner sitting on a mattress. There were two others they did not recognize.

"Hello," said Hef. "This is my wife, Crystal, my brother, Keith, and his wife, Caya."

"Nice to meet you all," said Bill.

"A pleasure to meet you," said Delilah.

"You're just in time for backgammon," said Hef.

# The Winner's Perspective

Dan drove toward a harbor. When he got there he parked his car. The sun shined on the small town. He left his car and walked toward the docks. Boats of all kinds were parked there, but they were not in good condition. Dirt and algae were on them. He searched the boats for a key but found nothing. The sun went down and the moon rose. The stars were vivid in the sky. He took a blanket from his car and slept in a boat. At night he heard the screams of the infected.

When he woke up he searched the buildings for supplies. He came across canned food and water in the supermarket. He got back in his car and left the harbor for a dirt trail. He reached a campsite. At the front was a house. He parked his car and went inside. The smell of rotted flesh filled his nostrils. He looked around but saw nothing. He walked up to a closet and the smell was more pungent. He opened the door and found a dead dog. He looked around the house and found a leash. He put the leash on the dog's collar and dragged the dog beside the bed. He sat down on the mattress. The sound of a car roared up the dirt path. He looked out the window.

A blood-stained RV drove past his car. The RV stopped and the driver got out. He had a Mohawk and wore human bones around his neck.

*Cannibal*, thought Dan.

The driver looked at the direction sign. A woman was in the back of the RV.

"Help me," she said.

She banged on the side of the RV. She opened the window to the bathroom, crawled out, and dropped to the ground. She was so emaciated she could not run. Two men walked out of the car. One was fat and the other very skinny. The three of them walked toward her. She stood up and wrestled the man with a mohawk. She managed to take his gun. She pointed it at the three of them as she stepped away.

"Come on, missy," said the fat one. "What are you going to do with that?"

The man with the mohawk pounced at her. The other two followed suit. She shot the man with the mohawk in the chest. She then fell on her back but as she fell she shot the fat one in the belly. When she was on her back the last one put up his hands.

"Now, there's no need for that," he said. "You go that way and I'll take the car and leave."

She shot him in the chest. The fat man sat on the ground and coughed up blood. She pointed the gun at his head and fired. She got back in the RV and drove away from the campsite.

Dan left the house with the dog in tow. He placed the dog in the passenger seat and drove back to the harbor. He sat in his car with the sun still out.

"Two plus two equals four," said Dan. "George Washington was the first president of the United States of America. A, B, C, D, E, F, G, H, I, J, K, L, M, N, O, P, Q, R, S, T, U, V, W, X, Y and Z. Now I know my ABCs, next time won't you sing with me? My mother's name was Laurie. My father's name was Bill. I'm not married. I have no children. My sister's name is Lucy."

Night fell. He got out of the car and went to the passenger door. He opened the door and brought the dog outside.

"Okay. We're ready now. We're ready to die. Come take us."

There was silence.

"Come on, now. It's our time to go. Me and my dog here have had an amazing time traveling across the country but we're ready now."

There was more silence. He walked into the store closest to his car. The place was dark. He went back to his car and got a flashlight. He looked around. He was inside a bar. He dragged the dog beside a stool, went behind the bar and took a bottle of rum and a shot glass. He sat down on the stool and started drinking. After ten shots he stumbled through the streets.

"You know, I'm a hero. I've survived the apocalypse. I've furthered the survival of the human race. Who can say that? Not one of you. Not you. Not you. Not you. No one. That's because I'm the best. That's right. In the zombie apocalypse only the strong survive and I was the strongest. I made it. I should get a fucking medal. I should get the girls. I should have more alcohol because I am the best. I deserve it. All I need now is a woman. I got all the luxuries except for that. I have food, I have drink, and now all I need is a woman. Shit, it's basically owed to me."

He stumbled back into the bar. He looked at the pictures on the wall. They were pictures of a family.

"The weak." He spit at the pictures. "You think you can survive with a family? You think you can live with a family? Not today, buddy. It is survival of the fittest and only the weak have families. I haven't seen one survive yet. I've seen children running through the streets alone but I've never seen a whole family make it. It's archaic is what it is. It's downright pathetic. To think they had hope."

He looked closer at the pictures in front of him.

"Is that…"

There was a picture of a man and his dog. They were both smiling. A lake was behind them and a small fishing boat was beside the dock.

"I've forgotten what it's like to love. It's been so long. I don't know what to feel anymore. I made it, but I'm as good as dead. Here I sit on a throne. The world open to me. The world letting me take whatever I want from it and I have nothing."

He stumbled to his car. He opened the glove compartment. There was a gun inside. He moved the gun out of the way and took out a photo. He looked at the photo of him and his dog smiling. They were in his backyard. He had short brown hair. During the infection his hair became long and mangled. His beard covered his face and mouth. He moved to the bar. He put his picture up next to the other photo.

He thought about when he drove his dog during the zombie infection. They would go to small towns, on the outskirts and he would send his dog in to search for trouble. If there were zombies he would bark. If the area was clear the dog would come back and lick Dan's hand. The dog's coat was golden in the sunlight as he went inside the ghost town's tavern. A rifle shot rang through the air and Dan heard his dog whine. That was the last time he ever saw him. Dan looked at the photos on the wall. He took the decayed corpse and placed it outside the bar. He turned around, walked inside the bar, and fell asleep.

He woke up the next morning. He walked outside. A woman stood in the middle of the road. He thought he recognized her from somewhere.

"Miss? Hello?"

She kept her head down. He walked over to her with his gun.

"Get the fuck up."

She looked up at him. Her face was dry. She was skin and bones. He knew he had seen her before.

"You're the girl. The girl from the RV."

She fell over to her side. The sun beat her down. She could not move.

"Give me a second."

He grabbed water and brought it back to her. He poured it into her mouth. She coughed some of it back up.

"We're going to bring you back, okay? Okay, all right."

He pulled her up and held her on his back. He brought her into the bar.

"Drink up now, you hear?"

She eventually came to.

"Where am I?"

"I don't know where exactly here is. What's your name?"

"Sarah."

"I saw you before. You shot those cannibals."

She backed up suddenly and looked around.

"I'm not a cannibal, if that's what you're wondering. I'm just trying to find shelter."

"Who are you?" she asked.

"My name is Dan. I used to work in accounting before the shit hit the fan. I was a fairly decent guy. I had a good job and a good girlfriend. I had a dog named Biscuit who was my pride and joy. I don't know if I'm scaring you more or less."

She looked around her.

"Less. My name is Sarah and I'm not your fucking problem. You don't know me. Thank you for the water, but I think I should be going now."

She started to walk out the door.

"I have food."

She stopped.

"It's canned so you know it's good. It looks like you haven't eaten in weeks."

"I guess I could stay for a meal."

"Perfect. What should I make you? We got chili, beans, corn and asparagus."

"I guess I'll have the chili."

"Chili coming up."

He handed her a can of chili.

"You know usually I don't like strangers because all they want is food, but I like you," he said.

"I like you too, Dan. You aren't so bad, after all. But look—what I was saying before. I should probably..."

"It'd be rude to just leave with the food. Let's sit here, eat and enjoy ourselves. You can go afterward, I swear."

"Okay," she sniffled. She coughed into the food. "Thanks."

They dug in. When the food was gone she stood up.

"I guess it's time for me to leave."

"You could stay the night. I haven't had company in a while. It'd really make my night."

"I should really be going."

"Okay, then."

She left the bar and he sat down on the stool. He sighed.

"I almost had a pretty girl. I almost remembered what it was like to be human again."

He ran out of the bar.

"Hey, miss."

She turned around.

"I got whiskey."

She smiled.

"Oh, what the hell."

She walked back up to him.

"I might as well enjoy my night." She walked back into the bar.

That night they got wasted and made love. In the morning he woke up before her. She lay on her stomach. He touched her arm and noticed something—a rash. It looked as if teeth had bitten her. The gash was severely infected. He hadn't noticed last night in the dark. He poked her again.

"Sarah wake up. There's something wrong with your—"

She turned around. Her eyes were dilated red. Her face was white as a ghost. She looked like a corpse with eyes of fire. She lunged at him. He backed up. She was on top of him. He flipped her over and held down her hands. He went for his pistol in his pocket but one of her arms came loose. She grabbed his wrist and brought it to her mouth. She bit down. He screamed and grabbed his gun. He shot her through the head.

"Fuck."

He searched her pockets and found keys to a boat called *Clementine*. He ran down the dock looking for the boat's name. When he found it he put all his food and water in the back of the boat. He put the key in the ignition. The boat rumbled but it did not start. He tried again. The same thing happened. He tried one more time and the boat started. He found a first-aid kit on the boat and put a bandage around his arm. He sailed forward. After three hours he saw an island. He covered the bandage with his long-sleeved shirt. The island had people living on it. They looked at him curiously. He imagined a new life there. A fresh start.

# Z

Bradford, Leah, Farrington, Stone, Kyle and Kaylie all sat in the lobby of Lone Mountain. In the midst of charades, they heard a noise outside the building. They looked out of the window and saw a pack of motorcyclists. A man with a black bandanna and white beard pushed the elevator button. Stone had the power turned off so no one could enter.

"We need to hide," said Stone. "Bring the guns."

They pushed over the blockade in the main hallway made of mattresses and crossed over to the next building. They hid in the cafeteria. The bikers kicked in the stairwell door and made their ascent. They soon reached a barricade made of box springs and climbed over them.

"They're in the building," said Farrington.

The box springs were not made to stop humans. The bandits looked around at the food stacked in the lobby.

"It looks like whoever was here isn't here anymore," said one of the bandits.

"Or they're hiding. They want it to look that way," said the bandit with the black bandanna. "Check the rooms."

Seven bandits moved toward the dorm rooms. The others picked up the food and brought the cans to their bikes.

"The rooms are clear," one of the bandits said.

"Good," said the bandit with the black bandanna. "Let's move out."

They left the school and the students listened as the bikers drove away.

"We need to prepare if they come again. We'll need to fight them," said Bradford.

"We can't take them on," said Stone. "There are at least 30 of them and eight of us."

"Bradford is right," said Leah. "We'll have positional advantage and we'll be out of food if they come here again. It's either us or them."

They rebuilt the two barricades and kept a lookout when night fell. At two in the morning the building's lights turned on. All the dorm rooms lit up. They all looked outside their rooms.

"The power is back on," said Stone.

"But how?" asked Leah.

"I don't know," said Stone.

"I know exactly what that means," said Farrington.

He went to his dorm room and closed the door. An hour later Stone knocked on the door.

"Farrington?" said Stone.

"Yeah," said Farrington.

"What are you doing in there?" said Stone.

Farrington opened the door.

"Come in and be quiet," said Farrington.

In his dorm room was a beanbag chair, a bottle of whiskey and a television. A game console was connected to the television.

"It's the new, well was the new *DK V*." Said Farrington. "I just got it before the infection hit."

"*DK V*?" said Stone.

"*Drive and Kill Five*," said Farrington.

Suddenly, they heard helicopters overhead. They both ran to Farrington's window and looked above them. Green military helicopters circled the school. They landed just outside the campus. Military personnel ran out of the back of the helicopters with guns pointed. They shot the infected that ran at them. Suddenly Farrington and Stone heard the elevator. They ran out of the dorm room.

"What's going on?" asked Stone.

"The military is here. An officer is at the elevator. He probably wants to speak with us," said Bradford.

They all looked at the elevator doors in anticipation. They opened and inside was a sergeant with two soldiers beside him.

"We heard there were survivors," said the sergeant. "We got your little radio call about a week ago."

The sergeant had a finely cut white mustache. He had good posture and was five foot six.

"So," said the sergeant. "It's in the interest of the United States to decontaminate the area and reinstate Trinity College. We've got students and professors on the helicopters ready to go. The Army will eradicate the zombie threat and then we'll leave you to it. Oh, and we want you to speak on the first day of school. Here is a summary of the school curriculum."

Stone took the paper. Bradford looked out the window. Students with bags and backpacks exited the choppers. They started going into the dorms.

"The war is almost over, boys. It's time to take back America," said the sergeant.

"Hell yeah," said Stone.

They all smiled.

"Yay," said Leah.

"One of you will talk to the students tomorrow morning. Let them know the campus and where the different departments work," said the sergeant.

"Okay," said Stone.

"I'll be going, then."

He went into the elevator and the infantrymen followed. He pressed a button and the elevator closed. The Army helicopters left. Night fell over the city. In the morning the students gathered at the center of campus. They had on backpacks and held rifles at their sides. There were at least 100 students.

"Welcome back. I know we've all been through a lot, but we survived and we must go on," said Stone. "We're here to learn and get our diplomas."

The crowd talked among themselves. They then looked back at Stone and the original six. Leah, Farrington, Kaylie, Kyle and Bradford all stood side by side.

"But things are not like they used to be. We need to create a new history. We need to tell the world about our story of survival. The curriculum will include the infection."

The sounds of motorcycles could be heard. The students looked around them.

"There are bandits here who want to murder us for no reason other than killing. They don't want money but I'm sure they want women. This is our university now. This is our home. Are they going to take that from us?"

"Hell no," yelled one student.

The rest shouted.

"Let's take back what's ours."

They all moved to the front of the school. The motorcyclists were parked outside. The students started shooting at them. The motorcyclists took cover behind their bikes or behind cars in the parking lot, but the wave of students was too large. The bikers' aim was terrible. Some tried to get back on their bikes and ride away but were shot down before they could leave. Others stayed behind cover and fired blindly into the crowd. The students pushed forward until they were on top of the bikers. No one escaped alive.

After the battle the original six went back to their dorms. Night was overhead and they went to sleep. The campus, however, was alive and well. The lights were on and people socialized.

The next morning classes started. Stone went to his English class, where he decided to accumulate survivor stories from around the state and turn them into a book. He would leave on a military helicopter tomorrow. In class Bradford worked on writing a book about the history of the zombie infection.

That night Leah and Stone had dinner. The restaurant on campus was Italian and the tables had candles on them for lighting. Stone looked over and noticed Bradford was in the restaurant, too. He was with a new friend he had made named Jeremiah.

"I'm so happy to be learning again," said Stone.

"I know," said Leah.

"But I have some terrible news," said Stone. "I heard of a student here who was pregnant. The mother died as she gave birth to an infected child and we don't know why."

"I heard about that, too," said Leah.

"Have you heard about the husband?" asked Stone.

"No," said Leah.

"They say he's on some new drug called Z and maybe that's the cause," said Stone.

"What's Z?" asked Leah.

"It's a low dose of zombie blood. It is not enough to infect you but just enough to make you go into an angry trance," said Stone.

"Jesus," said Leah.

They finished eating and went back to their dorm rooms. The next morning Stone woke up to the sound of a gunshot. He looked out the window. The shooter was a student. Other students had killed the armed gunman by the time Stone ran down the stairs with his M16. He looked at the body.

"Who is he?" asked Stone.

"He's the husband of that pregnant chick," said another student.

Stone and other students placed the body off campus.

"That's one thing you don't get used to," said the student.

He walked back with Stone.

"What's that?"

"The smell of rotting flesh."

A military helicopter landed near the campus. Kyle and Stone went into the chopper.

"What are you leaving for?" asked Stone.

"I'm marketing for a pharmaceutical company named Merricorp," said Kyle.

"Oh, yeah. Those guys who created the cure for the infection, right?"

"Yeah, what are you doing?"

"I'm documenting peoples' lives. Stories of survival and heroism."

"Oh, cool. Good luck," said Kyle.

"Thanks, man."

The bird left the ground and flew toward Washington, D.C. When Kyle reached Merricorp headquarters people led him to the CEO's office.

"Hello, there, Mr. Warner," said Joe.

"Nice to meet you, sir," said Kyle.

"We are all very excited to have you on board. Your record is stellar, to say the least. You worked in New York. Is that correct?"

"Yes, yes, that's true."

"And you were unemployed shortly before the infection. Is that right?"

"The economy was not doing so well."

"Well, I can look past all that. But tell me, Kyle. I can read a person like a book, so I already know the answer, but I want to hear it from you. Can I trust you? Are you a trustworthy guy?"

"Yes. Of course."

"Good, good. I knew you were like that." He laughed. He had a cigar in his mouth. He was overweight and beads of sweat were on his forehead.

"So you won't mind any discrepancies or moral misdoings on our part, right? You wouldn't care. You're one of us now. Come here. I want to show you something."

He led Kyle to the elevator and pushed 13. The doors closed. When they opened they were in a large room that looked like a warehouse.

"This is where we produce Merricorp's famous Z cure."

There were conveyor belts with liquid being poured into bottles.

"You see, Kyle. Here at Merricorp we're like family. We share everything."

"Uh huh."

"You want to know a secret, Kyle?"

"Sure."

"We orchestrated the zombie infection. We wanted it to happen so we could cure the population. You see, it's very capitalistic in nature. We create a problem that only we can solve and then we make money."

Kyle was still.

"You see, we never wanted anyone to die. It sort of, well, got out of our control." He smiled. "But we lived through it and survived. There is one more thing I want to show you."

They went back into the elevator. Joe pushed G for garage. The elevator went down. The doors opened to trucks with boxes inside of them.

"This is our second and more discreet side of your marketing venture. We sell Z. Have you heard of it?"

Kyle was frightened. It was as if he had been thrown into a different reality. He was not familiar with his surroundings. Everything seemed different.

"Yes."

He looked into Joe's eyes.

"Good. Well, it's not your normal marketing job but we want people on the streets to hear about it. We want them to think highly of this product. Do you understand?"

"I do."

He was slowly fitting in. Fitting in to his new reality.